All She Wants

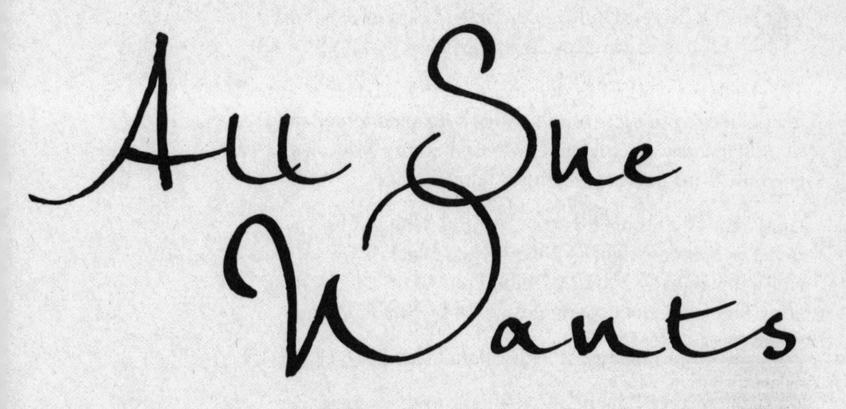

JAID BLACK
DOMINIQUE ADAIR
SHILOH WALKER

POCKET BOOKS
New York London Toronto Sydney

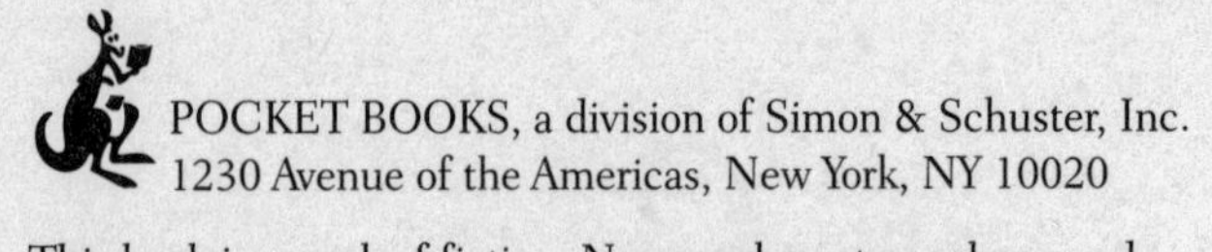

POCKET BOOKS, a division of Simon & Schuster, Inc.
1230 Avenue of the Americas, New York, NY 10020

Published by arrangement with Ellora's Cave Publishing, Inc.

ISBN-13: 978-1-4165-3505-8
ISBN-10: 1-4165-3505-5

This Pocket Books trade paperback edition November 2006

10 9 8 7 6 5 4 3 2 1

Manufactured in the United States of America

Contents

Adam & Evil

Jaid Black

One

"May I be blunt?"

"Can I stop you?"

"No."

"Then by all means . . ."

Julia Cameron's gaze narrowed thoughtfully as she deigned to engage in eye contact with her father's protégé. Forty-year-old Samuel Adam was the man her father wanted her to date and, as he'd told her in no uncertain terms, eventually marry. It was just like the old goat to attempt to force someone into her life who was so much like himself.

A rigid, unsmiling, tyrannical, emotionally frigid robot who no doubt bled oil in lieu of blood.

Thanks, Dad, but no thanks.

At thirty-one, Julia was unlikely to change. If she ever settled down—a very tentative if—it would be with a sensitive soul of a male. The sort of guy who didn't cower away from his feelings, worrying that such a show of vulnerability was emasculating. He would be everything that, God love him, her father had never been.

"I'm waiting," Samuel murmured, his voice measured.

A feral smile enveloped her face as she chose her words carefully. Everything about the man was even-keeled and firmly in control. His dark hair was perfectly cropped just above the ears, his suit impeccable wool and cashmere herringbone. He'd probably never raised his voice to anyone in his entire life. He didn't have to. Those intense green eyes and that stoic face innately commanded respect. The son of a bitch needed to be rattled.

"You are, without a doubt, the biggest jackass I've ever had the displeasure of sitting next to on an airplane," Julia told him.

A lie, perhaps, but better to make him hate her and leave her alone than lead the guy on. Pointing to a bottle of Samuel Adams brand beer that a passenger an aisle over was drinking, she batted her eyelashes.

"Furthermore, your name is one S away from being appalling. Samuel Adam? You sound like a drink, for heaven's sake!" She waved a hand magnanimously in the air between them. "I wouldn't date you if you were the last man on earth. No offense."

"None taken."

Julia frowned at the casual amusement in his tone. That wasn't the reaction she'd been going for. Men tended to become angry and feel aggrieved in such a situation. She'd been down this road many times before and had thought she knew the terrain.

Apparently robots didn't possess the same reactions as the average male.

"Well, good," Julia said dumbly, treading down unfamiliar territory. She rustled the newspaper on her lap. "Now if you'll excuse me, I'd like to finish reading this riveting piece on, uh . . ."

She took a quick glance down, having no idea of the contents. Her father published it, but she never read it. ". . . this riveting piece on the life of slugs."

More amusement. He didn't smile, but his eyes glittered. The knowing in those light green orbs reminded her of a stalking jungle cat, an analogy that made her swallow a bit roughly.

Samuel Adam might sound like an alcoholic drink, but his demeanor was sobering. Nothing got to him. No one intimidated him.

Ever.

"I wouldn't dream of keeping you from reading such an engrossing article."

Her glower would have killed a lesser man.

"In fact," Samuel said, steepling his fingertips, "I'm impressed." His eyebrows rose slightly. "I didn't know Barbie dolls could read. Your father must be very proud."

A Barbie? *Her?* Julia didn't know whether to laugh or take offense. Apparently beer-boy had failed to notice the extra twenty-five pounds on her five-foot six-inch frame. Or her J-Lo bootie. Or her very red and curly, non-blond hair. Or the doctorate hanging on her office wall.

Her teeth snapped together. He was just trying to get back at her, prod her into making a scene so he'd feel better. Damn, he was good. Almost, but not quite, a worthy adversary.

"He's very proud," Julia assured him, feigning inordinate fascination with the article on slugs. Why had her father published this boring shit? It was the daily paper, not a journal for science geeks, for crying out loud. "I am, after all, nothing if not amazing."

"Mmm yes. As remarkable as a talking marionette."

Her teeth ground together, but she would not take the bait. She would rise above and stay a step ahead. She would—

Why the fuck is beer-boy lifting my arms over my head?

"No strings attached," Samuel reflected. He looked genuinely intrigued. "Interesting."

There were many comebacks to be had, many acidic, witty replies to be made. Unfortunately, all of them were eluding her at the moment. "You've got brass balls," Julia huffed. "I'll give you that much. Nobody ever talks to me like that!" She sounded like a defiant little brat, but oh well.

"A pity," he said firmly, those intense eyes of his finding hers.

"Just what the hell does that mean? That people *should* talk to me with no respect?"

"It means you should get what you give," Samuel said calmly, rigidly. "If you belonged to me, I'd put you over my knee and spank your ass soundly."

She couldn't believe how outrageous his words were! Or how arousing. Julia twisted in her seat, coughing in her hand to cover up her discomfit.

Had she thought him to be almost, but not quite, a worthy adversary? She had been wrong. Samuel Adam was, in fact, the real deal. Such an opponent had to be taken seriously. This wasn't like the last poor schmuck her father had sent to court her—she doubted this guy would just walk away with his tail between his legs, afraid Julia would get him fired. No, Samuel realized he wouldn't be issued his walking papers from Cameron Publishing. If he did, he would be immediately snatched up by a rival company. The situation set panic alarms off in her mind.

She opened her mouth to rebut, but was cut off by an alarm of another kind. Julia's eyes widened as the lights in the airplane's cabin began rapidly flicking off and on, a shrill sound blaring over the intercom. Two flight attendants servicing the first-class cabin lost their balance, their bodies flung to the floor by the airplane's jarring motions.

"What's happening?" she breathed out, heartbeat accelerating. She clutched the arms of her chair with both hands, fingernails digging into the vinyl. What a day! "Are we crashing?"

"I don't know," Samuel replied evenly. His large, powerful hand covered hers as he assessed the situation. "But I won't let anything happen to you."

For some insane reason, Julia believed him. Her grasp on the seat tightened as a loud, trembling voice sounded over the intercom.

"All flight attendants and passengers prepare for an emergency landing."

"We're flying over the damn ocean!" Julia hysterically pointed out. "Where are we going to land? The welcome portal to the underwater kingdom of Atlantis?"

Oxygen masks dropped from the overhead bins before he could reply. She heard children crying from somewhere behind them back in the coach section. Her heart slammed against her chest as she fumbled with the mask, trying to secure it over her face.

A simple, routine flight from San Jose to New York. She had taken this very flight, no doubt on this very plane, dozens of times. Her family held estates in both Manhattan and Costa Rica, though Julia primarily resided in the latter.

Samuel had shown up at her doorstep two days ago under the guise of escorting her back home for the Christmas holiday. *Her father-trying-to-set-her-up-with-another-robot* radar had immediately flown sky-high. She was, after all, thirty-one, not three. She hadn't required escorts for years.

There had been something different about Samuel Adam from the first moment he'd entered her tropical refuge, some enigmatic mystique that gave her pause. He radiated an aura of control and power that no one could fake—a man either possessed it or he didn't. Samuel oozed it.

After two days of playing mouse to his cat, Julia had been more than grateful to take the flight back to the States with her father's protégé. Anything to eventually ditch him. He was getting under her skin, and that would not do. Nothing got to the man, nothing cowered him. If she hadn't been so hell-bent on loathing him, she would have admired him.

He wanted her money. He wanted to control Cameron Publishing. All men saw her as a means to an end.

The movie screens in the cabin turned on, snapping Julia back to the moment. An emergency landing instruction video began to play. The two actors smiled serenely as they calmly placed the masks in front of their faces, then lifted the attached rubber bands to position them behind their heads.

Oh right! What a realistic reenactment! As if anyone could be that tranquil when they were about to die. Oscar-potential candidates the actors were not. They should be hyperventilating, screaming, and possibly clawing out their own bulging eyes.

Julia's head began to swirl, dizziness engulfing her. She hadn't figured out the mask yet and wasn't getting enough oxygen.

Two strong hands held up her quickly slumping body. The mask made its way to her face. Oxygen returned. Julia stared up at Samuel with wide blue eyes.

"I have to go help in the back," he said from behind his own mask. "You'll be okay, Julia. I promise."

A selfish gene whispered to her that she should beg him to stay, to not leave her here to die alone. But she knew those kids back there needed him much more than a grown woman did. She might be a lot of things, but egocentric wasn't one of them, despite what she'd led Samuel to believe.

Besides, she could take care of herself. She'd always done as much. Growing up motherless with a workaholic father did that to a person. If there was one lesson Julia had learned early in life, it was the futility in waiting on a man to rescue her.

She nodded her head. "I'll be fine," she said in a monotone, her brain still relatively scattered from the previous lack of oxygen. "Go to the children. They need you."

Two

Separated from the other survivors, they'd been drifting for two days. Almost out of food, Julia had predicted several times that they were goners. Samuel, on the other hand, was his typically arrogant, in-control self.

"We'll be fine, Julia," Sam stated. She watched his muscles tense from the strain of continuous swimming. "We've made it this far and we're still alive."

She snorted, but kept swimming. They were alone in the middle of the ocean. They hadn't so much as spotted another ship. Their stash of airline peanuts, bottled water, and something resembling stale pretzels was nearly gone. Sunburn covered all of Julia's pale body and half of Samuel's bronzed one. Despite all that, he persisted in his mentality. Robots—faithful to their preprogramming until the end.

Landing, if one could call it that, had been a nightmare. Unbelievably, none of the passengers died at impact. As it turned out, the emergency landing video was on target and the seats really did morph into flotation devices. All might have ended well had a thick, disorienting fog not enveloped the area. One night they were floating next to the other fatigued passengers and, a short nap later, they were bobbing alone in the middle of the torrid ocean.

Christmas was less than a week away. There would be no turkey, ham, and trimmings this year. The way things were looking, and the way sharks kept circling from below, the only thing on the menu this holiday season would be raw human à la Julia and Samuel.

A dark shadow glided by. A dorsal fin emerged, then quickly retreated into the water. Heart pounding, Julia held on tightly to the pocketknife Samuel had given her.

"Why don't they just eat us and be done with it?" Julia panted, swimming vigorously. She couldn't recall ever being this frightened or her nerves ever being so frayed. That was saying a lot when you were the daughter of a man who possessed more enemies than friends. "They're toying with us."

"They don't know what to make of us so they're waiting for us to weaken," Samuel told her matter-of-factly, "to show some sign of vulnerability."

Great. "Like?"

"Difficulty swimming. Fresh blood from a wound . . ."

Julia mentally counted the days since her last menstrual cycle. She hysterically hoped she'd remain on schedule.

". . . anything that tells them we are vulnerable prey."

Silence.

She lapsed into contemplative thought, her life playing like a DVD before her mind's eye. She still had a lot of things left to do before she died—accomplishments to achieve, Mr. Right to find and marry, babies to make with said man. She wasn't ready to become shark sushi.

Dr. Julia Elise Cameron was a world-renowned botanist. She

knew her tropical plants like nobody's business. A thousand specimens of the same variety could be facing her and she could still tell them apart for the individual organisms that they were. They were distinct and vibrant beings to her, full of life and love. And, unlike people, easy to comfortably surround herself with.

When it came to interacting with her own species, Julia had always come up short. She could blame her father's lack of attention, or the death of her mother at the tender age of six, but there was no sense in casting blame anywhere besides at her own two feet. She was a grown woman, had been for more years than she wished to contemplate, and her life was what she'd made it.

Julia was, and would probably die being, the horticultural version of an old maid with cats. The thought was more depressing than it should have been. Men had come and gone over the years, of course, but nobody she could envision living out the rest of her life with.

Aside from the usual courtships of high school, her first real love had been Phillipe, the artist she'd met during her junior year in college at the Sorbonne in Paris, France. Phillipe had been dashing and charming, not to mention an excellent lover. He excelled at the art of lovemaking and Julia quickly figured out why—she'd met politicians who were more faithful.

For graduate school she left the Sorbonne and Paris behind and headed back to the States. Once a fine arts major, she completed the prerequisite courses to pursue her next degree in botany, this time at New York University. At NYU she met Randy, a drama student. Randy had been Phillipe's spiritual twin, minus the French accent.

Tired of men and their cheating, disloyal ways, Julia had converted to lesbianism—or tried to anyway. Jenny had been beautiful, any lesbian's dream come true, but when it had come time for Julia to return the sexual favors Jenny had bestowed her with . . .

She winced at the memory. As much as she might wish it otherwise, going down on another woman was simply not Julia's thing. Trying to fake her way through it, she'd held her breath and desperately attempted to make her almost-lover come.

Had it not been for the fact that Julia needed to come back up for air and take a deep, gasping breath before recommencing, she and Jenny might still be together, damn it. The submersible whale technique went over about as well with Jenny as rice cakes at an all-you-can-eat pancake breakfast.

Picky people.

Following the Jenny fiasco, Julia had abandoned any realistic hope of finding true love and concentrated instead on her plants. Her father sent the occasional suitor over to test the proverbial dating waters, but she was having none of that. Her dad might be a revered and powerful publishing magnate, but he was hopeless when it came to two things—expressing emotions and picking out a would-be son-in-law.

Samuel wasn't the first hopeful to catch her father's eye, though admittedly he was turning out to be the hardest to shake loose. What neither man seemed capable of fathoming was that the year was 2006, not 1506. She didn't want an arranged, polite marriage, where the husband ruled supreme and the wife smiled and hosted dumb tea parties. She wanted passion and emotions, a meeting and merging of the soul and mind—the very things that Samuel, so like her father, could never give.

Samuel Adam was powerful in the publishing world, a rising star that would never dim. He made deals that affected many lives and raked in money using his Midas touch. He was handsome and dominant, controlled and together. He was everything a woman should want in a husband, but also all the things Julia knew from the experience of growing up with a man so much like him, didn't really make for a happy marriage.

Her mother had died alone and embittered. It was no way for a woman to leave this world.

Deep down inside, there was an untypical part of her that still held on to the elusive dream of finding happiness with a man, but over the years that part had shrunk to the point of nonexistence. Or it had, anyway, until death came knocking.

Here in the middle of the ocean, with predators just a bite away from killing her, life flashed before Julia's eyes and smacked her upside the head with its ironies. She needed to survive. She still had a lot of things left to do. Samuel wasn't the one to do them with, but he deserved to live, too.

Just when the hope of survival all but deserted her, just when she thought it was time to succumb to the fatigue, a small spot of . . . something . . . snagged her peripheral vision. Was it? Could it be?

"Oh my God," Julia breathed out.

"What?" Samuel asked. His tone was urgent. "Are you all right? Have you been bitten?"

She blinked. His voice sounded almost . . . well, *human*. Just a small hint of emotion, yet detectable nevertheless. Perhaps that happened to robots in moments of extreme duress.

"No," Julia assured him. "I'm fine." A smile enveloped her full lips as she jerked her head to the right, indicating what lurked just a few miles away. "We've found land."

Everything in Samuel Ian Adam's life was perfectly ordered and under his firm control. It was the way it had always been, it was the way he had envisioned it always being. When he told someone to jump, they asked him how high. When he issued a command, it was obeyed immediately and without question. When it came to matters of business and winning, not even his boss, William Cameron III, thought to gainsay him.

Sam preferred the status quo. He relished order and logic. He thrived on being the smartest, the calmest, the most methodical and calculating.

And then *she* came along.

When his business mentor had asked him to fly down to Costa Rica and collect his only child for the holidays, Sam immediately recognized that the task was no ordinary quest. William's sole heir was unmarried, Sam was still a bachelor. It was, logically speaking, a good marriage match. Sam would run Cameron Publishing, William would retire, and Julia would be well taken care of. Completely sound reasoning.

Nothing about Julia Cameron was sound, let alone reasonable.

Just getting past the Costa Rican estate's butler had been a lesson in restraint. When Sam had announced to Jorge that he'd been sent by William to collect Julia, the servant had feigned having no working knowledge of the English language. Sam had proceeded to trump that ace by requesting Julia's presence *en Español*. All that had earned him was the door getting slammed in his face.

Sam's teeth gritted from the insult, but he hadn't given up. He knocked on the double doors again. And again, and again, and again.

From the moment the irritating female with the bouncy red curls had thrust open the doors and clapped blue eyes on him, Sam had understood this task would be no easy feat. He should have received the message at some point during the Jorge incident, but nothing could have prepared him for one Dr. Julia Elise Cameron.

A half-empty bottle of Chianti in one hand, a dying plant in the other, and an expression on her face that said somehow in her strange world those two things went together, she calmly asked him, "Who the fuck are you and why are you breathing on my doorstep?"

She was crass and rude, obnoxious and sarcastic. She cared more about her plants than people and thought nothing of dismissing him as an inconsequential weed that needed to be ripped from her garden. She was everything he didn't want in a wife. Sam had never been angrier.

Or more intrigued.

Given Julia's general surly temperament, his arousal toward the tiny woman was baffling. She might not have been short exactly, but when standing next to his own six feet three inches, she barely made it up to his chin.

It wasn't Julia's looks that caused him to covet her, though she was certainly beautiful in an exotic sort of way. She had bright blue eyes that spoke of an angelic side she was far from possessing, red hair as fiery and vibrant as her take-no-prisoners attitude, skin as creamy and translucent as a doll's, and a body with bumps and curves in all the right places.

And yet it wasn't her level of attractiveness that was pushing his buttons and getting under his skin. It wasn't her money or even the key she wielded to Cameron Publishing. Sam almost wished it was one of those things. It would be easier to admit to. Much easier than acknowledging it was the she-beast's *I-am-independent-woman-hear-me-roar* demeanor that had his cock so hard.

He was swimming in a pool of sharks and still had a hard-on. He wished that particular part of his anatomy would roll over and play dead, because he wasn't in the mood to have it bitten off. No, Julia would enjoy his newly emasculated state with a bit too much relish. He wouldn't let her get away from being beneath him in a bed that easily.

Rigidly and devoutly old-fashioned, Sam long aspired to marrying the twenty-first-century version of June Cleaver. June had made for the perfect wife. Ward and the kids had always been her foremost concern. Supper was prepared and ready when her man came home from a long workday. She was docile and submissive, smiling and cordial—everything a wife should be.

Everything Julia wasn't.

"I can't believe it!" Julia announced, her excitement uncontrollable. Sam blinked, his thoughts clearing. "Land, ho! Land, ho! Land, ho!" she rejoiced.

Her girlish giggles forced him to swallow a bit excessively. She was more than beautiful when she laughed so exuberantly. She was downright gorgeous.

There went his damn cock again. He frowned, not at all happy with his body's reaction to a woman who could give prickly lessons to a cactus. Another two miles of swimming and at least he wouldn't have to worry about his dick becoming a shark banquet.

"I see it," Sam confirmed. "Hopefully it's inhabited."

Another two miles and they'd reach land. After that they'd search for food and civilization.

And after that he'd fuck Dr. Julia Elise Cameron out of his system . . . literally.

Three

"I DON'T BELIEVE THIS!" Julia wailed, enraged hands flying every which way. "We swam for *days*. We defied all the odds—not to mention multiple flesh-eating predators—only to meet with long, hideously torturous deaths via starvation and dehydration!"

Sam sighed. A bit dramatic, perhaps, yet to the point.

"Look at this place! It's barren! Completely and utterly dried up!"

He couldn't deny her words. Somewhere in the middle of the Caribbean they might be, yet they had managed to find refuge on the one small dot of an island lacking a lush, tropical landscape. The place resembled the Sahara more than a jungle.

"Don't you have anything to say, beer-boy?" Julia gritted out. Her nostrils flared as she stalked toward him, soaked red hair flinging madly. She put her arms out in front of her and walked like Frankenstein's monster—or a robot, he wasn't certain which. "Does death compute?" she asked in a computerized monotone. "Does death compute?"

Despite the horrible circumstance they were currently in, or the fact that William Cameron III's daughter was a modern-day

Nellie à la *Little House on the Prairie,* Sam found her imitation of him slightly amusing. Enough so that he had to snort at her.

"Yes," he replied in the same droid monotone. "It does compute."

Julia's eyes rounded. Her mouth went agape. And then she did something he wished she hadn't—she threw her head back and laughed.

He grunted. When she was happy, she looked far too beautiful for his peace of mind.

After the plane went down and swimming for their lives became grim necessity, Julia had been forced to shed all her clothing, except for the shirt and transparent g-string she was wearing. Standing on dry land, the wet, white cotton plastered against her, nothing was left to Sam's virile imagination. Her large breasts were capped off with big, stiff nipples, and her red pussy hair had been trimmed into a small, barely there, triangle.

Sam coughed into his hand and glanced away. He looked to the sky and mentally counted to ten, trying to dampen his quickly arousing spirits.

"Touché," Julia chuckled. "So one of my father's clones possesses something resembling a sense of humor. Who'd a-thunk it?" She shook her head and grinned. "I certainly didn't think so when he telephoned to say you were coming to San Jose to, and I quote, 'retrieve' me."

Sam's eyebrows rose as she gave him her back. Julia was busy visually scanning the horizon, but he was preoccupied with what she'd just said. And with the full, round, slightly sunburned bottom that now faced him. *Jesus H. Christ.*

He shook his head to clear it. In a nutshell, Julia had known he was coming for her, which explained her nasty behavior at the front doors to the estate. Sam also got the feeling that he wasn't the first suitor William had sent down to Costa Rica—a fact that made him feel a jealousy he didn't have the right to.

Julia's head cocked to the left. Her nose began to twitch as it made sniff-sniff sounds. Sam frowned, uncertain what to make of such bizarre, primitive behavior.

"I smell *Saccharum officinarum,*" Julia announced.

She sniffed again, letting her nose lead her off to the left toward hilly terrain. She resembled a hound dog ferreting out prey. Frustrated, and beginning to wonder if Julia'd been raised by a pack of wolves with outrageously delicious bodies, Sam ran an agitated hand through his damp hair and followed.

"Saccharum officinarum?" he bellowed. "What the hell is that? Where are you going?"

Julia stopped in her tracks. She hesitated, then whirled around and looked at him dumbly. "Did you just raise your voice to me?"

Sam's nostrils flared. "Yes. I did," he bit out, his temper boiling just below the surface. Everything was getting to him—*she* was getting to him. Costa Rica. Jorge. The plane crash. Swimming with hungry sharks. Being stranded on a deserted island with Julia the she-wolf. Her luscious ass, ripe nipples, and the teasing shadow of pussy hair he could faintly make out . . .

The woman could conjure up pieces of his personality he'd thought never to unleash on another. "You were sniffing the air and you're insane!" he yelled. "Your father is insane! Everybody with the last name of Cameron is, in fact, insane! And what the hell is *Saccharum officinarum*?"

Her lips hitched up into a half-smile. She studied him as one would a nonrepresentational piece of art—not certain what she was looking at, but somewhat intrigued by it. He could only grunt at her. The woman was odd.

"*Saccharum officinarum* is the scientific name for sugar cane," Julia said with uncharacteristic patience. "I can smell it and I'm going to find it so we don't starve to death. Come on, Samuel."

The dominant alpha male in Sam wanted to provide for Julia, not the other way around. Yet surprisingly, and contrary to his *Leave It to Beaver*–ingrained belief system, he found himself impressed by and proud of the sexy botanist.

He clamped a hand to his forehead. Surely he had taken a fever. She was burrowed under his skin farther than a giant, blood-sucking tick. Next she would try to possess his soul; she would dance around a campfire as she ripped it out with forceps in hand and a sinister smile on her face.

She was evil. Wicked, vile, and Satan-spawned.

He needed to fuck her so bad his balls had gone blue.

"Fine," Sam growled, scowling at her. "Let's go find it."

His muscles tensed as he prepared to hunt. He *would* make it out of the jungle with his mind still intact. And, come hell or high water—most likely hell—Julia *would* become his June. If he was honest with himself, he'd considered her to be his before he'd even set off for Costa Rica to acquire her. Sam had no intention of devolving into one of those tree-hugging, soft, beta types in the name of peace . . . Julia would have to do that. Oh, he'd be considerate, even give in to her wants when he felt it logically appropriate, but that was where the line in the sand would be drawn.

She might not realize he'd staked a claim on her yet, but she would soon enough.

"By the way," he told her, his gaze continually straying back down to what he wanted to brand, "call me Sam."

The part of the island they'd swum up to was a barren no-man's-land, but just over the hill lay paradise. A luscious, tropical landscape bursting with banana trees, sugar cane, coconuts, and assorted vegetation and wildlife beckoned with their untainted scents and sounds. Julia breathed deeply. The life inherent to the jungle habitat was intoxicating.

"God, this is beautiful," she whispered aloud, not really talking to anyone. "This is the way it's supposed to be."

Leafy, green plant life. Birds painted from vibrant colors. The sounds of monkeys screeching, calling out to each other in an intricate language their kind understood.

Julia sensed Samuel—Sam—staring at her, so she blinked and turned away. She wasn't certain what to make of the man and therefore didn't know how to behave around him. Usually it was a simple matter of being as bitchy as humanly possible until the would-be suitor scurried off. Stranded in the middle of nowhere, ditching Sam wasn't even a remote possibility. She hadn't been able to shed him even before the plane went down. Now?

"I better make us a shelter," Sam announced, inclining his head westward. "A thunderstorm is imminent, maybe just a few hours off."

Julia followed his line of vision. Indeed, he was correct. Black clouds had coalesced over the ocean, barely audible cracks of thunder in the remote distance. A storm was coming—and it looked like a bad one.

"I'll help you," Julia insisted.

"It would be far more helpful," Sam said firmly, "if you gathered us together a few days' worth of food instead. We don't know how long the storm will last. It could be days."

She narrowed her eyes at him. "Are you trying to make a bitch out of me?"

"A what?"

"A bitch." She waved a hand. "You know, one of those female types who cook, clean, and listen to every word a man says as though it's the gospel truth." Her chin notched up. "I don't cook, I don't clean, you don't know jackshit, and I am perfectly capable of building a shelter."

His leopard eyes flared, then raked over her body. She shivered despite her efforts not to be affected by him. He kept staring at her intimate places in a way that made her think he coveted them. Men like him typically preferred sticks with boob implants, not voluptuously built women.

"Eventually I *will* make a 'bitch' out of you, as you so eloquently put it," Sam told her in his usual calm tone.

She gasped.

"But not right now. At this moment we need two things—food and shelter. You are the botanist. It only makes sense for you to collect the food, as I don't recognize anything around here other than the bananas and coconuts."

Julia hated to admit it, but the man had a point.

"I do, however," Sam continued, "recognize the bamboo and the fact I have a knife to cut it down with."

Her forehead wrinkled. "How did you get that past security at the airport anyway?"

He shrugged. "I didn't. Another passenger did. I found it when we were in the water scavenging for food and kept it just in case this situation arose."

Very resourceful. There went that damn sense of admiration toward him again. Even amid a crisis, Sam had been thinking ahead.

Julia relented. "Oh, all right, damn it. I'll give in and be the bitch this time," she grumbled. She stomped off deeper into the jungle. "But next time it's your turn, Mr. Adam."

Four

THEY LOCATED A CAVE, scared out the local wildlife, and claimed it for their own use. Sam hadn't finished tying the last knot on the makeshift bamboo door when the storm erupted, bringing a torrential downpour with it. He quickly built a small fire inside the tiny alcove, but it wasn't enough to warm her chilled bones. Cold and shivering, her shirt and panties still drenched, Julia searched for something—anything—that could double as dry clothing.

She sighed, defeated. Unless Sam knew how to make bamboo dresses, she was screwed.

"Take your clothes off," a husky voice said from behind her, "before you catch a cold."

Julia's blue eyes widened. Her heart pounded against her breasts. "I-I'll be all right," she stammered out, refusing to face him until her breathing returned to normal. "Just give me a moment."

Silence ensued as her teeth chattered. She could feel Sam's stare boring into her back, flicking over her ass cheeks.

"If you can't take care of yourself properly, Dr. Cameron," Sam told her, "then I'll be forced to take matters into my own hands."

She whirled around to face him. Sweet lord, he was staring her down like he was a leopard and she was his lunch. His dark hair was still damp, the color in strict contrast to the jade of his predator's eyes. His tanned body was covered in only the boxing shorts he'd had on under his jeans when the plane went down, his erection stiff and poking against the material.

"Matters?" she asked nervously. "Or me?"

Their gazes clashed and held. His eyes were intense, on fire.

He didn't answer the question. "Take off your clothes," Sam said thickly.

Her breathing labored, Julia's body responded to his words even as her brain screamed to stay far, far away from him. Her belly clenched in a knot of pure arousal and her nipples stabbed against the wet fabric of her shirt.

"This is a very bad idea," she whispered, her voice hitching.

His lips alleged nothing, but his eyes said it all. Once Sam had her, he had no intention of letting her escape his clutches. Julia took an instinctive step back. The tiny cave began to feel smaller. He took a step toward her. Her breathing, already dense, grew heavier.

"Take off your clothes," Sam again instructed, his tone dominant. His heavily muscled body tensed, prepared. "I won't have you catching a cold and taking ill."

The soaked clothing *was* making her teeth rattle. Still, she didn't think standing naked in front of her father's protégé was a good idea.

"*Now,* Julia."

His commanding tone was more erotic than it should have been. She didn't want to feel aroused in his presence, but she was. She hesitated for a moment.

As if it was inevitable, Julia brought her fingers to the hem of her shirt and began pulling it up. Her large breasts got caught in the tight fabric, but she jiggled them loose and tugged the garment up over her head. A purr sounded from deep in Sam's throat as she took it off and let it fall to the ground.

"Good girl," Sam praised her, his eyelids heavy as his gaze seared her hard nipples. "Now the rest."

A hand at either hip, Julia took her panties off inch by inch. She pushed them down below her knees, straightened up, and kicked them the rest of the way off. Sneaking a look at Sam, she saw that his stare was zeroed in on the thatch of damp red curls between her thighs.

"You're a very good girl when you want to be," he murmured. "Aren't you, Julia?"

She said nothing as he looked his fill at her naked body.

"Come here," Sam instructed, reaching out to take her hand. "Let's warm you up by the fire."

Julia doubted the necessity of the fire. Her skin, once cold, tingled with heat and sensual stimulation.

Sam led her to the fire and turned her around to face it. Situating himself behind her, his two strong hands slid between her arms and sides and cupped her breasts. Julia whimpered as he began kneading them, his thumbs massaging her stiff nipples.

"I'll get my tits nice and warm," Sam growled low into the whorl of her ear. From somewhere in the back of her lust-drunk mind, she recognized that he was already referring to her private parts as his property. "I can't wait to suck on my nipples, baby."

Julia's breathing came out in ragged pants. She was already dangerously close to coming.

She thought to tell him to stop. The words never made it past her lips.

Julia moaned as she reveled in the intimate breast massage. She instinctively ground her hips at him, her ass pressing against his iron-hard erection.

"Do you feel what these tits and that ass do to my cock, sweetheart?" Sam murmured into her ear.

She was so damned close to coming. Just a little more stimulation would throw her over the edge.

Sam's hands glided down her body, to her pussy. He sifted his fingers through the intimate curls. "Open your legs wider," he told her. "I need to dry the hair on my cunt."

Julia obeyed immediately, more turned on than she'd thought humanly possible. Her pulse worked triple-time as he played with her pussy lips, massaging them like he had her breasts. Moments later, his fingers found her clit. Her heartbeat went into overdrive.

"Come for me," Sam commanded, a man used to getting what he wanted. He vigorously massaged her clit, rubbing it in brisk circles. She threw her head back against his solid chest and groaned. "Come, Julia."

One hand played with her pussy, the other went back to massaging her breasts. His fingers tugged at her nipples, rubbed her clit. She bucked against him, the knot of arousal in her stomach aching to break loose.

"Sam."

The coil in Julia's belly burst into a violent orgasm. She wailed out her pleasure, the sound echoing throughout the cave. Breathing heavily, her knees like rubbery noodles, she sank to the ground of the cave, thankful that Sam had the forethought to catch her.

"Very sexy," he hoarsely praised her. "You're so beautiful."

Not really, but he made her feel that way. When he held her like this, touched her like this, looked at her as though she was the most sensual woman on planet Earth . . .

He made her wish they weren't so wretchedly alike. Opposites attract and opposites they were definitely not. He was an alpha male, she an alpha female. They were both stubborn and strong-willed, determined and relentless. If they wanted something, they took it, more's the pity for any who stood in their way.

Including, she dejectedly conceded, each other.

Julia could only hope that her father rescued her before it was too late. Namely, before Samuel Ian Adam got under her skin so deeply that there would be no hope of getting him out.

Help was bound to come sooner or later and Sam found himself hoping for later. Out there in the real world, he doubted Julia's ability to tolerate him for very long. He could shove his will down her throat and hope it took, but for the first time in his life, he didn't know if it would work.

Julia complicated his life, his very belief system. She was everything a man reared by a domineering, nagging mother didn't want. Independent, strong-willed, and feisty, she gave as good as she got. She didn't need a man and could do just fine on her own.

But is that independence and fire the same thing you've spent a lifetime despising?

He didn't know. He didn't want to analyze it. For once in his calculating life, Sam wanted to revel in the here and now, in the moment and in the woman.

One thing was for certain—even if Julia proved to be a dominatrix outside of the bedroom, she was mouthwateringly submissive inside of it. He had commanded her to sit on a specific rock and play with her nipples while he watched. She had obeyed without hesitation.

Sam pulled off his boxer shorts and stood over Julia from where she sat on a flat stone. Her eyes widened when she looked at his cock—a reaction he loved. He casually seated himself on an adjacent rock, then issued his next instruction.

"Spread your legs wider," Sam told her. "I want to see all of my delicious cunt." Julia paused and began to comply. "I didn't say you could stop massaging my nipples," he told her. "Tug on them while you open your thighs for me."

"I need to play with my clit," Julia gasped. *"Please, Sam."*

She wanted to come, he wasn't ready for her to . . . yet.

"Did I say you could play with my cunt?"

"No."

"Then keep tugging on those stiff nipples."

She moaned, but complied. Sam was enjoying the sensual game, but didn't know how much longer he or his cock could withstand it. Watching Julia play with her nipples was the most erotic thing he'd ever seen. The areolas were light pink, the nipples dusky rose. Gazing at her tight cunt made him wonder just how much of a squeeze it would give him. It also gave him the craving to find out what that sweet pussy below the red curls tasted like.

"You've got great tits, Julia," Sam murmured. "Or should I say, *I* have got great tits."

She moaned as she continued to tweak her nipples.

A drop of pre-cum dripped from Sam's cock. He had to touch her, play with her, fuck her.

"Stand up and walk over to me," he ordered her. "Tug those nipples harder while you do it."

Julia's nipples were so stiff. Her eyes were glazed over with unquenched pleasure. She walked over to where he sat, two big tits dangling in front of his face.

"Put your hands at your sides," Sam purred. "Don't move a finger without my permission. Do you understand?"

"Yes."

He lifted an arrogant eyebrow. God, he couldn't wait to feast on those nipples. "Yes, *what*?"

Julia looked confused.

"Yes, *sir,*" he clarified for her.

She cleared her throat. For a moment, Sam thought she would balk at his command. But then, making his cock swell just that much more, she surprised him.

"Yes, sir," Julia whispered.

Her breasts heaved up and down in time with her labored breathing. His gaze was mesmerized by her luscious tits. So big and plump. He couldn't recall ever seeing nipples quite that erect.

Sam grabbed her tits like he owned them, and as far as he was concerned he did. Julia gasped as he popped one stiff nipple into his mouth and sucked it like he meant to brand it. Unable to decide which nipple he wanted to suck on more, he palmed her tits as close together as they could go and feverishly sucked one and then the other in fast, ruthless motions. Back and forth. Left one and right one. Over and over. Again and again. Her breath came out in a rush.

"That feels so good," Julia whimpered. "That feels so good, sir," she quickly amended.

She was learning the sex game at an astute rate. An A+ student, Sam decided.

He dragged his mouth away from her breasts, releasing the

left nipple with a popping sound. He ran greedy hands all over her naked body, wanting to touch her everywhere.

"Spread your pussy lips," Sam growled.

She immediately obeyed. Pale, trembling fingers eased apart her sexy cunt lips, revealing the erect clit and tight hole he was more than ready to claim.

Sam shoved his tongue up her cunt hole, moaning from the exquisite taste and tightness.

Fucking her would be better than heaven.

He tongue-fucked her for several minutes, his thumb playing with her slippery clit. Julia's body began to shake and he knew she was close to coming. Sam went in for the kill.

Slipping his hands around her to knead her ass cheeks, his lips found her clit and drew it into the heat of his mouth. He sucked on the sensitive bud hard, his cock aching from the sound of her moans.

"Yes-sir-yes-sir-yes-sir!" Julia wailed, not permitted to so much as buck her hips. *"I'm coming, sir."*

Julia screamed as she came, a violent burst that covered his lips in feminine juices. Sam panted as he tore his mouth away from her delicious cunt and, standing up, issued another order.

"Get on the ground and kneel on all fours," he said in a tone that broached no argument. "I want to see my tits dangling, my ass raised up in the air, and my cunt on display."

"Yes, sir," Julia said thickly as she took to the cave's floor.

She sprawled her body out, belly down, so that her weight rested on her knees and hands. Looking up at him from over her shoulder, long, red, curly hair so much an aphrodisiac, she waited like the perfect, sweet submissive for her man to take what belonged to him.

Damn, she was sexier than any woman had a right to be. That plump ass might not always be in vogue, but it had always been a lure to Sam. He could see her tight cunt hole pouting from between her splayed pussy lips, and big tits dangling just beyond her taut belly.

Sam palmed her ass cheeks, spread them apart, and guided his cock to her wet entrance. Perspiration dotted his forehead. Every muscle in his body tensed in preparation. "Beg me to fuck you," he gritted out.

"Please fuck me, sir," Julia begged, gasping for breath. She was as aroused as he was. "Please, sir—please fuck me."

He sank into her tight, sticky cunt on a growl, impaling himself to the hilt. Julia moaned as he fucked her, his cock mercilessly pounding in and out of her flesh. He took her like a possessive animal, riding her hard, telling her with every thrust that she was his.

"Sam," she gasped, her tits jiggling beneath her, her hips meeting him thrust for thrust. "Sam—oh God!"

He took her harder and deeper, faster and more ferociously. He sank into Julia's tight pussy over and over, again and again, glutting himself on her cunt. She moaned and fucked him back, the sound of flesh slapping flesh reverberating throughout the cave. The scent of their combined stimulation permeated the air, further arousing him.

"My cunt feels so good," Sam ground out. His nostrils flared, jaw tensed. "Oh shit—*Julia*—baby."

Her pussy sucked his cock back in with every outstroke. The sound and feel of the tugging was excruciatingly erotic. Sam fucked her harder, faster, his fingers finding her hips and digging into the flesh there. In and out. Over and over. Once. Twice. Three times more . . .

He came on a roar, every muscle in his body simultaneously tightening and releasing. Julia continued to throw her pussy back at him, milking him of every drop of cum he had to give.

Their breathing mutually ragged, their bodies slick with sweat, Sam stood up and held his hand out to Julia. She accepted, letting him lead her closer to the fire where they could warm up.

A distant boom of thunder sounded outside the cave, telling them the terrible storm was moving on. In all the excitement of having sex with Julia, Sam had forgotten about the storm. He turned his gaze back to Julia.

She rubbed her hands together in front of the fire, a sad smile on her face. It was as if she had already decided that, just like in Vegas, what happened in the cave would forever stay in the cave.

Sam closed his eyes briefly, not wanting to deal with reality. When he opened them, he turned to her, wanting her to forget all the obstacles between them. His mouth came down and covered hers, his kisses deep and meaningful. Julia's tongue darted out and dueled with his. Sam groaned and pulled her closer, his erection stabbing against her belly.

She kissed him back with all the passion she had inside. And in contrast to the robot Julia had thought him to be, his intensity matched, perhaps even exceeded, her own.

The sound of a helicopter flying overhead pierced the quiet. Julia broke their kiss, dragging her full lips away from his. She glanced up at the ceiling, then back to Sam. They both knew what the sound meant without needing to go outside to visually confirm it.

They had been rescued. Reality had returned.

five

Julia had hoped and prayed her father would rescue her before Samuel Adam got too deeply under her skin. Her dad had, in fact, found her. She just wasn't certain about the last part of her wish.

The helicopter ride back to civilization was a quiet one. Samuel sat across from her, his gaze trained on her, his expression brooding. Julia stared out the chopper's window, attempting to sort out her tumultuous thoughts.

What she had shared with Sam during those stolen moments in the cave wasn't soon forgotten. The part of Julia long accustomed to keeping men at bay beckoned her to distance herself from the man seated across from her, the one as rigidly domineering as her father. He wouldn't change—people were what they were—and she knew in her heart that she could never be the sweetly smiling, docile wife that men like Sam aspired to having.

While the sex games had been beyond amazing, Julia was and always had been fiercely independent. She didn't need a man to complete her, just to accept her and love her for the woman she was.

Sam needed oil but she was water, he needed night but she

was day. Try as she might, she couldn't fathom how a relationship between them could ever work. If her heart could accept what her mind already knew as gospel, she might be able to turn back into the porcupine and conjure up a few acerbic remarks to keep Sam at an emotional arm's length.

The irony being, she didn't want to hurt him either. Their time together had been short, but she had learned something important about the robot in those precious hours.

Sam bled red blood, not black oil. He showed a stoic face to the world, but he was simmering with passion and hot emotion just below the steel façade.

Julia took a deep breath and exhaled slowly, her gaze still fixated out the window. If she thought for even a second that there was a chance she and Sam could find a happily-ever-after, she'd jump at the opportunity. But Samuel Ian Adam needed something else—*someone* else.

He needed a woman that she could never be.

It wasn't in his nature to let what he wanted more than anything in this world just walk away. And yet Sam couldn't bring himself to chase Julia down, to force her to his side. If she came to him, it had to be willingly. His needs had to take a backseat to hers.

Sam watched Julia walk briskly from the helicopter and toward an awaiting limousine. Her vivacious red curls bounced with every step. He smiled. That hair was so much like the woman it decorated—uncontrollable, tenacious, and possessing a mind of its own.

Every primal fiber of his being demanded that he hunt Julia down and tell her she belonged to him. That's what men like Sam did—win at all costs. And he was confident that he *could* win. At least until she tired of him and his admittedly old-fashioned ways.

She might stay with him a day or even a year, but in the end she would walk away. Julia was a bright, blooming flower and Sam a mercilessly stagnant weed. For the first time in his life, he didn't feel good enough, worthy enough, to be in another's life. The realization was a jarring and humbling one.

As Sam watched the limousine whisk Julia away, one thing became crystal clear—his life, once perfectly ordered and under his firm control, would never be the same again. It was easy not to crave something you never had to begin with, but an entirely different animal when you lost it just after indulging in a sweet, unforgettable taste.

Julia deserved to be happy. She ought to have a man so much better than what he was.

Sam sighed as the truth hit him hard in the gut—he loved the woman. Loved her so much that he was letting her walk away into the sun, rather than pull her back into the shadows of his life.

He had to let her go. He just didn't know how to say goodbye.

Six

Julia sighed as she listened to her date drone on and on—and on and on and on—about his health problems. Had they been anything serious, like cancer or heart troubles, she would have sympathized. Acne on his chest and chronic athlete's foot were disgusting, but hardly life-threatening. Nor were they topics any polite person would broach during Christmas Eve dinner, and in front of their date's father no less.

Sam never would have behaved so boorishly during a family meal. He would have been well mannered, engaged everyone in interesting conversation, and, she thought, as she eyed her date's tattered T-shirt and military fatigue pants, properly dressed for the occasion.

Julia had met Dan over a year ago and while she'd been impressed with his artistic abilities and sensitive nature, she hadn't really been interested enough to date him. Yesterday Dan had been bicycling by—sans the tattered T-shirt—when Julia's limo pulled up in front of her father's estate. He waved her down and asked her out again. This time she accepted, figuring there was no time like the present to start working Sam out of her system.

Dan was cute, sensitive, and concerned with the world

around him. He was everything Julia had aspired to in a life-mate. He was also, unfortunately, about as interesting as watching paint dry.

"Sorry to hear about the acne," William Cameron III intoned. He frowned at Julia, then looked back to his plate. "Perhaps you should consider seeing a dermatologist."

"The medical community is rife with fraud," Dan countered, his voice passionate. Julia shrugged apologetically at her dad. "I wouldn't give a dime to those bastards!"

Her father didn't know what to say to that. Then again, she doubted any sane person would know what to say to that.

James, the Cameron butler, cleared his throat, thereby announcing his presence. Julia exuberantly welcomed the interruption. Her overly cheerful *save-me-James* smile told the butler all that he needed to know—an emergency of his concoction would transpire very soon and Dan would have to leave so Julia could attend to it. It was a system the duo had perfected over the years, and one that served her well.

Julia grunted but kept smiling when James seemed not to notice her plea for help. Instead, the butler inclined his head and announced the arrival of two additional guests—guests that Julia had no idea were invited.

James cleared his throat. "Mr. Samuel Adam and his date, Ms. Felicia Marit."

Julia's smile faded as she watched the impeccably dressed Samuel Ian Adam enter the room, a stunning blonde bombshell at his arm. She flashed her father an angry look, but like James, he pretended not to notice.

Sam's gaze clashed with Julia's. He glanced at her date, back to her, then looked to William. "Thank you for the invitation, sir," he said with the politesse of his breeding. He handed Julia's father a bottle of vintage wine. "I'm pleased to accept it on behalf of Felicia and myself. This is your favorite Merlot. I hope you enjoy it."

William stood and accepted the bottle, then invited the two new arrivals to be seated. "I will." He flashed Sam a grin. "Please join us."

Julia's nostrils flared. Her heartbeat accelerated as she envisioned herself lunging at the other woman from across the table and tearing her hair out. Had Sam made love to her already? Had he forgotten about their time in the cave this quickly?

Sam looked wonderful today, his dark hair perfectly cropped above the ears, his cologne an English scent, his suit an Italian one. His jungle cat green eyes, intense and commanding, were trained on Felicia.

She hoped the bitch gave him a venereal disease. Or two or three or ten.

"Well," her father announced, "now that we're all here, it's time to eat."

"I've tried Chinese herbal remedies to no avail," Dan whined. "I went to Haiti and sought out a cure from a voodoo priestess." His fist thumped down on the table. Julia winced. "I can't get those fucking pimples off my chest no matter what I do!"

"Ever considered Clearasil?" Sam asked drolly. He couldn't believe Julia preferred a pathetic imbecile of a man like that over him! Had the acne-ridden little son of a bitch fucked his woman? God, he hated him. "I hear it works wonders."

"The medical community is a farce!" Dan bellowed. "A sham, a travesty, and a money-hungry . . ."

Sam cocked an eyebrow and looked at Julia while her date prattled on. She cleared her throat and glanced away.

"So," Julia said, interrupting Dan mid-diatribe. "Tell us about yourself, Felicia. How did you meet Sam? What do you do for a living?"

Sam winced. This was a path he wished Julia hadn't taken them down. Once Felicia started talking about her work, she couldn't seem to stop.

Felicia beamed. "I've known Sammy for over a year and he finally asked me out! I work at the makeup counter of a major department store," she told everyone in her bubbly cheerleader tones. "Cosmetics are my life! One day I hope to have my own line of mascara."

"Why stop at mascara?" Julia asked sardonically. She waved a hand about the room. "Conquer the world and have your own line of lipstick, too."

"Excellent idea!" Felicia enthused. Her beaming smile faltered as she looked to Sam for guidance. "Sammy, what do you think about that? Would mascara *and* lipstick be taking on too much?"

"Do enlighten us with your makeup wisdom, Sammy," Julia said with her she-wolf smile. "We women have trouble thinking for ourselves."

William cleared his throat, thankfully sparing him the need to reply. Sam glared at Julia from across the table. She blinked several times in rapid succession, a false angelic smile plastered on her lips.

"So," William said, turning his attention to Sam and Felicia, "how will you two spend the holiday tomorrow?"

"However he wants to," Felicia chirped.

"I'm Jewish," Sam said bluntly. "I'll spend it working."

Or hunting Dan down and killing him with his own bare hands. Either scenario held equal allure.

"You're Jewish?" Felicia breathed out. "You don't celebrate Christmas?"

"No."

That gave her a moment's pause. But then, like any good June Cleaver, she quickly recovered. "It's okay, Sammy. I'll convert."

Julia rolled her eyes. Sam coughed into his hand, willing the red in his face to go down.

Had he thought this was what he wanted? A woman who agreed with everything he said? A woman who held no higher purpose outside of being whatever it was a man wanted her to be?

In the words of his dear departed grandmother, *Oy vey.*

"If everyone will excuse me," Julia said as she stood up, "I'm not feeling very well."

"Julia—" William began.

She flashed everyone a quick smile, but ignored her father. "Please enjoy the meal."

Thrusting open the window in her bedroom, Julia delighted in the feel of the cold New York air hitting her in the face. She breathed it in, her breath swirling like curls of smoke around her.

She had known what kind of wife Sam wanted. She just hadn't expected to be faced with it—with *her*—so soon after leaving the island.

The doors to her bedroom opened and closed behind her. Julia sighed, not bothering to turn around.

"Forget it, Dad," she said without glancing back. "I'm not hungry. This dinner was *your* great idea so *you* can deal with it."

He said nothing.

"Give Ken and Barbie my warm regards," Julia said sarcastically. "And tell Dan I'll call him later."

"You better not call him later," a dangerous voice growled from behind her. Heart thumping, Julia whirled around. "I'm serious, Julia," Sam said, prowling toward her. His eyes were narrowed, angry. "This has gone far enough."

Sam! Oh God, I've missed you!

"I'll call anyone I want to," Julia sniffed, her chin notching up. "It's my life and I run it! Go develop that mascara line with Mensa-girl. But be prepared. When she realizes there are several shades of the stuff, it'll probably throw her into a mental meltdown!"

Sam's lips twisted into a mask of fury. "Have fun scouring the world for a cure for acne with Giorgio Armani!" he roared. "God forbid the idiot go down to the local drugstore and let 'the man' fuck him over with a cheap tube of Clearasil!"

Julia's nostrils flared. "I hope your newly converted Jewish wife feeds you nonkosher meals every day of your wretched life!"

"May Acne-Man never find a cure and you're forced to pop his pimples for him as a prelude to sex!"

Julia gasped. "Samuel Ian Adam, that is gross!"

"Did you fuck him?" Sam gritted out, closing the gap between them. His eyes glittered territorially as he cupped her pussy in one hand through the fabric of her red dress. "Did you give him what's mine?"

"No!" she fumed, pushing his hand away. Jaw clenching, she grabbed Sam's cock through his trousers. "What about this? Does it need to be cut off? Did you fuck her brains out? Because she sure doesn't have any to think with!"

"No, I didn't," he hissed.

"This is mine," Julia growled, unzipping his trousers. "If you ever give it to another woman I'll hunt you down, whack it off, and feed it to one of my carnivorous plants!"

"You are evil," Sam said huskily as she went to her knees and began sucking him off. His fingers threaded through her hair. "God, I love you."

"Iwubewtoo," Julia announced from around his cock.

"Huh?"

She popped it out long enough to clarify, "I love you, too."

Sam groaned as she sucked on his cock like a lollipop. His balls tightened as she bobbed her head ferociously back and forth, his breath coming out in pants. The sound of her mouth sucking him in aroused her. The way he pulled her hair tightly and forced her face toward his hungry cock made her wet and eager for him.

"I'm coming," Sam ground out, holding onto her hair by the roots. "Oh shit—damn. *Julia.*"

He burst on a groan, his cock jerking in her mouth as he came. Julia drank all of him, relishing every last drop. She had missed him so much.

Sam was everything she had never wanted in a husband. Julia was everything he had never wanted in a wife. And yet as he drew her into his embrace and they held each other with all the love and passion they possessed, she knew they'd both found their happily-ever-after.

Julia had once thought that she and Sam were too alike for their own good. After all, according to the old cliché, it's opposites that attract. What the cliché failed to mention, however, was that while opposites may attract, it's similars who stick together.

Holly

DOMINIQUE ADAIR

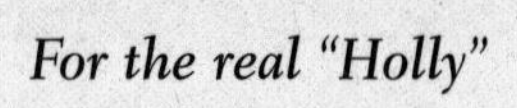
For the real "Holly"

Prologue

It's about time!

Footsteps sounded on the steps alerting Holly to the return of her Master. She rubbed her nose against the padded leather spanking bench that supported her upper torso. How long had she been handcuffed to this dratted thing? One hour? Two? More?

Raising her head, she tried to arch her back, anything to work the kink from her upper spine and shoulders. The handcuffs rattled against the steel bench legs, restricting her movement to only a few inches. Her ankles were also secured to the bench, leaving her legs spread and her sex exposed and vulnerable to whoever might walk into the room.

On most occasions, this only added to the excitement of bondage games. Tonight was a rare exception.

After attending a disastrous bondage party scene in the French Quarter, they'd returned to Greg's house, where he'd immediately escorted her downstairs to his dungeon. He'd ordered her to remove her clothing before cuffing her to the spanking bench, then left her alone with her thoughts.

She sighed and rested her chin against the bench. To say she was conflicted would be an understatement. In their time together they'd attended many scenes but never had he commanded her to have sex with one of his friends. Holly realized this was a common request between Masters and slaves, though it was one she'd never considered he would make of her.

When they'd begun their relationship little more than a year ago, she'd made it clear to him that while she craved bondage, she drew the line at engaging in sexual relations with strangers. There were only a few things she wouldn't do for her Master and that was number one on her list.

Up until tonight her choice had never been challenged, as Greg had respected her wishes. She bit her lower lip. Holly had no idea why he'd decided to issue the request in front of a roomful of partygoers, as he had to have known what her response would be. True, he'd drunk quite a bit this evening and he was upset over something that had gone wrong at work, but that was no excuse to violate their relationship boundaries in such a manner.

Needless to say she'd refused, though she had tried to minimize the embarrassment for him as much as possible. When he'd refused to yield to her wishes, she'd been forced to stand her ground and create a bit of a scene before he'd agreed to leave with her.

It would be an understatement to say that Greg was angry with her for disobeying him publicly, and she wasn't terribly happy with him for making the request in the first place.

Maybe it was time to rethink the boundaries of their relationship.

The door opened and Greg entered the dungeon. Dressed in black slacks and a loose-fitting white shirt, his sandy-blond hair was tousled as if the wind had played havoc with it. His handsome face was set in stern lines as he walked toward her, his gait purposeful. In his hand he carried a cocktail glass, Dewar's on the rocks, no doubt.

"You haven't been a very obedient slave lately, Holly."

"I'm sorry, Master." She kept her voice contrite. Even though she was irritated with him for his earlier request and for keeping her bound for so long, her body knew this particular game well. A soft ache blossomed between her thighs.

"I've spoiled you, ruined you, in fact. Once you were the perfect submissive and lately I've grown lax with your training." The clink of ice against the glass sounded as he swirled the amber liquid. "This is evidenced by your impudent behavior this evening."

Her chin came off the bench. "Impudent? I never meant—"

"Silence, whore!" He slapped her across the cheek so hard she bit her tongue.

The taste of blood permeated her mouth and Holly stifled a moan, shocked to her very core. Her cheek burning, she stared up at her lover. What in the devil had gotten into him? They'd played some very explicit role-playing games but he'd never resorted to calling her names or striking her across the face. Had he lost his mind?

"How could you humiliate me like that?" He was standing so close to her that she could smell the liquor on his breath, and his voice rose with each word. "You refused a direct order from your Master in front of my friends. Now they'll believe I'm weak, that I've been lenient with my slave." He tossed back the contents of the glass.

"Master, you know how I feel about having sex with a stranger." She shook her head. The taste of blood was making her nauseous. "I just can't do it."

He lifted his arm and flung the glass against the wall, where it shattered. She winced when glass shards struck the back of her bare legs.

"You've accepted me as your Master and I will decide what you will do and with whom you will do it. Do you hear me, slave?"

Her stomach roiled and she spat blood and saliva onto the tile floor. He had lost his mind.

Greg walked to a table where a variety of bondage implements were arranged. "I will flay the arrogant flesh from your bottom and remind you that it is I who calls the shots in this relationship." He picked up a short-handled whip. "You've bound yourself to me, you are mine to command. You will be made to obey."

He's drunk.

Panicked, Holly rattled the cuffs against the legs of the bench. "I don't think this is a good idea. Please release me and we'll talk about this."

"You don't need to think, whore. That's my job." He gave her a dark look—anger blazed in the depths of his eyes. Laying his hand on her back, he walked around the foot of the bench and out of her line of sight. Broken crystal crunched beneath his shoes.

I no longer trust him . . .

Her skin crawled where he'd touched her. "You've been drinking, Greg." She rattled the cuffs louder this time. "I want out of here. Release me this instant."

"You're mine, Holly." His tone was singsong. "It doesn't matter what you want, as you're here to serve me. My pleasure will be yours."

She heard the whistle of descent just moments before the whip struck across her buttocks. Her body jerked in response and she bit her lip as pain licked over her skin, leaving a trail of fire in its wake.

"Greg—"

She yelped when the second blow landed and she sank her teeth into her lower lip until she drew blood. Before tonight, he'd never dared to strike her this hard. Her mind scrambled for an escape but there was none at hand. His house was secluded and it didn't matter how loud she screamed, as the nearest neighbor was almost a mile away. Her only recourse was to use her safe word before he went too far . . .

"Eleanor!"

Her body braced for a lash that never fell. For a moment, she was still, her spine tight and her breathing harsh. Silence. After a few moments she allowed her forehead to come to rest against the bench. Her breath came in harsh gulps and her skin was slick with sweat.

It was over, it was over.

"Bitch," Greg snarled. "Don't you dare try to command me—"

Without warning the whip fell again. She screamed, her body bowed against the pain.

"Eleanor!"

This time the blows continued and soon her buttocks and thighs were burning. Tears fell in earnest now. No matter how loud she screamed, the whip continued its fiery caress until her mind went hazy with the pain. Her muscles strained, the cuffs dug into her skin, though she knew she could never get free on her own. She was truly at his mercy.

"Master," she sobbed.

"Shut up, whore."

Another lash tore at her skin and she jerked as if he'd touched her with a cattle prod. Sobbing, she sagged against the bench, her knees refusing to support her weight any longer. Behind her she heard the whip fall to the floor and she shuddered. Something wet ran down the back of her leg.

"You drove me to this." Greg's breathing was ragged and he grabbed her by the hips. "You have no one to blame but yourself."

She heard the rasp of his zipper and that was enough to jerk her out of her pain-induced delirium. She thrashed against her bonds, desperate to free herself and escape the dungeon.

"Don't do this, Greg. I'll never forgive you." Her voice was hoarse and her throat ached from her screams.

His laugh was hollow and her heart dropped into the pit of her stomach.

"I don't need your forgiveness. You seem to keep forgetting that you're my slave and I can do with you what I will."

His fingers sank into her flesh and she began to scream.

One

Eight months later

"You've got to be joking."

Aghast, Holly stared at the man who'd been her friend for the past seven years. Doug Mains was pushing fifty, though he didn't look a day over thirty-eight. Always well groomed, today he wore a perfectly tailored black suit with a crisp white shirt and a blood-red silk tie. His still-blond hair—he saw his hairdresser religiously every three weeks—was combed back from his handsome face. Even now she was aware of the admiring looks he received from other women in the restaurant.

"I would never joke about something like this, Holly." Doug's chocolate-brown gaze was sympathetic. "With the rising interest rates and the skyrocketing prices for properties in the French Quarter, we felt we couldn't turn it down. The economy is slow, our sales numbers were down for the past two quarters, and we have to make up for it somewhere." He gave a slight, embarrassed shrug. "Consequently we opted to sell the bulk of the mortgages we held in the Quarter and yours was one of them."

Her hand clenched the napkin in her lap. "You and Greg both promised me you'd notify me before any changes were made to our agreement—"

"I think, in the long run, you'll see this will work out in your favor," he continued, speaking as if she'd said nothing. "You should be receiving a letter in the next day or so outlining the details of the deal."

Irritated beyond words, Holly slapped her crumpled napkin on the table. "How can this be for my own good, Doug? You just sold my mortgage to a complete stranger who gave you the best price." She hissed. "Why didn't you just sell it to one of those vulture bookstore chains? I'm sure they'd love to have my location and you probably could've pocketed more profits that way."

He shook his head. "Now you know I'd never do that to you . . ."

"Oh look, scruples. I thought maybe you'd left those at home in your other suit." She crossed her arms over her chest, not caring if she sounded like a complete bitch. Even though his brother, Greg, had messed with her royally, she'd thought her relationship with Doug was still solid.

It appeared she was mistaken.

"Holly . . ." Doug's voice took on the tone that told her he wasn't pleased with her behavior. "This is business, not personal, and there is no need to be nasty or feel hurt about it. I had no choice but to sell the mortgages, as we're looking to expand our business. I told you months ago about our impending acquisition of the Braymen bank chain. This is a multimillion-dollar deal and we had to put quite a bit of cash down up front in order to get the deal we wanted. Unfortunately, thanks to the economy, our liquidity report wasn't quite up to snuff to get the loan at an acceptable rate and we were forced to liquidate a few properties for a quick influx of cash. It is regrettable that your property was included in the deal but we had to help our bottom line."

"But you know how much that building, my bookstore, means to me. I was so pleased when you and your brother agreed to our business loan arrangement because I thought I could trust you—" Her voice broke. Holly snatched up her napkin and spread it over her lap just to give her hands something to do. "You also know how that damned bookstore chain—"

"The one you call the Evil Empire?"

"That would be them and trust me, they deserve the name." The napkin knotted in her hands. "They've been after me, doing anything they can to try and drive me out of business so they can pick at my corpse. How do I know the new owner won't just up and sell my mortgage to them?"

Doug shook his head. "I don't think you have to worry about that, my dear." He picked up his knife and fork and began cutting his grilled salmon into neat, bite-sized pieces. "The sale negotiator asked quite a few questions about you on behalf of the new holder." His eyes glinted with amusement. "And most of them were personal questions, not just about the mortgage or the state of your business."

She relaxed her grip on the abused linen. "Why would a banker ask personal questions about me?" Holly's stomach turned when he speared a salmon cube and popped it into his mouth. Her exquisite Bourbon Street Chicken Salad lay in her stomach like lead and there was no way she could even think about eating any more. She pushed away her plate. That was too bad as it was a favored lunch and she hated to waste good food.

"Your mortgage wasn't bought by a banker." Grimacing, he poked at his rice until he'd unearthed a tiny sliver of hot pepper. He scooped it up and put it to the side where it wouldn't contaminate the rest of his lunch.

Her mama had always told her it wasn't natural for a Southerner to turn their nose up at spicy foods and to never trust anyone who did.

Score one for Mama.

"It was bought by a local company, Clarke & Sons. Their main business is importing furniture and goods from Europe and the East." He picked out another piece of hot pepper, the distaste on his face evident. "They are a conglomerate and one of their sidelines, Clarke Mortgage, specializes in real estate."

Holly picked up her wineglass. She usually confined herself to one glass at lunch but this day would be an exception. "How many mortgages did you sell to them?" She drained the glass and caught the eye of the wine steward to indicate she'd need a refill.

"Seven. They're based here in New Orleans and are looking to expand their business." Doug shrugged and speared another piece of salmon. "In this economy it's the smart thing to do. A growing company cannot be too careful or place all their faith in one line of business, as it'll spell disaster in the long run."

"Doug, why didn't you tell me about this before now? You and I have lunch at least every other week. There were ample opportunities to bring this up before today."

He didn't look up. "It was a spur of the moment decision—"

Holly's gaze slid over his immaculate appearance. With his

thousand-dollar suit and handmade Italian leather shoes, this was a man who didn't make a move until everything had been double- and triple-checked. It took him at least a half hour to place a simple restaurant order, or weeks of research before deciding on a vacation destination. Nothing was spur of the moment in his orderly, tight life.

"Even I know better than that. It takes weeks if not months to iron out a contract and proceed with a sale such as this." She gave her thanks to the wine steward, who'd arrived with a fresh glass.

Doug gave her a pained look. "Holly, I didn't want to worry you. I knew this was the best thing to do for my company. The business really did need some quick cash and since you and my brother are no longer involved in an intimate relationship . . ."

Holly's feet turned to ice. Greg. She should have known that bastard was behind the whole deal. That little weasel had been after blood ever since she'd kicked him out of her bed and her life. Struggling to remain calm, she placed her glass on the table. Her hand curled into a fist.

"Is that what this is about?" Her voice was low, hard. "My failed relationship with *The Bastard*?"

Doug looked distinctly uncomfortable and he gave up any pretense of eating his lunch. "He was devastated when you left him, Holly." He dabbed his lips with the napkin, a prissy movement that only served to irritate her more. "He is family and also my business partner. The fact is, he's quite bitter where you're concerned and I tried to dissuade him from this course of action as I knew you'd get hurt. He feels that you reneged on your promises to him—"

She leaned forward, her anger bubbling just below the surface. "I reneged? How did I renege?" She braced her elbows on the table. "Your brother whipped me so severely as to leave a scar across my lower back and buttocks." Her voice was sharp but she couldn't seem to help herself. "When we entered into our relationship, we made several agreements and one of the most important ones was that stop meant stop, not hit me harder."

"Holly, please—" Doug gave apologetic nods toward the tables nearest them. "Please lower your voice, you're making a scene."

Seething, Holly grabbed her glass of wine and polished it off. "Greg is an immature bastard and I must have been mentally ill to even have considered fucking him let alone take him on as my Master." She picked up her purse and rose. "You and I have known each other for a long time, Doug, and even though I am feeling betrayed right now, I still consider you a friend. As such it pains me to say this, but it is for *your* own good. Grow up and quit letting Greg run your life and your business. You can make your own decisions and it's about time to step out of his shadow and take charge of your life."

Doug gaped at her, his mouth opening and closing like a fish out of water. Feeling sick to her stomach at his lunchtime revelations and chugging the second glass of wine, Holly turned and headed for the door, panic nipping at her heels.

Doug was right about one thing—Greg had indeed sent her a letter.

Even though her hand was shaking, which made the print hard to read, she couldn't tear her gaze from the familiar cream-colored letterhead.

Dear Ms. Broussard,
This letter is to inform you that your mortgage has been sold to the mortgage firm Clarke Mortgage. This sale is nonnegotiable and should you have any questions, their contact information is located in the phone book.

Sincerely,
Greg Mains, CEO
Mains Mortgage & Trust

No doubt about it, her ex-lover was a cowardly bastard.

She choked back a bitter laugh and dropped the letter onto her cluttered desk. In the past eight months her ex-lover had done everything possible to try to win her back into his bed. He'd sent her hundreds of flowers and a mountain of expensive gifts, all of which ended up in the Dumpster.

Just a few weeks ago he'd become more persistent, and he'd taken to calling her at all hours of the day and night and arriving on her doorstep unannounced. When she failed to respond to his attempts at reconciliation, he'd hired a private detective to document her every move. Every time she'd stepped out the front door of her bookstore or her apartment above, she'd been aware of the man armed with a video camera who'd watched her from his nondescript midsize car across the street.

She'd been forced to change her phone number and keep her blinds drawn at all times. Late last week she'd gone to court and obtained a restraining order against both the detective and The Bastard.

Her gaze landed on the letter. She didn't buy Doug's explanation that the Mains brothers wanted to boost their earnings reports by selling off a few mortgages. She smelled Greg behind this deal. He knew he couldn't get to her any other way and he'd opted to strike at the heart of her life, her store. She sighed and rubbed her hand over her eyes. Even though they were at complete odds and the chances of their reconciling were nonexistent, it had never occurred to her that he'd try and take his frustrations out on her business. She wasn't nearly as devious as he.

Book Ends, the bookstore her parents had opened in the early sixties, meant everything to her. The three-hundred-year-old store building was paid off though it required a great deal of expensive maintenance. To Holly, it was worth every penny.

Even though she'd known Doug for years, she'd never met his brother until two years ago when she'd taken out a sizable mortgage from his family's bank to make improvements on her building. She'd found out after the fact that he'd granted her the loan at a minimal interest rate because he'd wanted her in his bed.

After using most of the money to upgrade the wiring and replace the roof and plumbing in the aging building, she and her junior partners had opted to expand the bookstore café with the balance. When they'd originally opened the café, they'd started out serving only coffee and desserts. After the expansion, the menu now boasted designer sandwiches and salads, and the larger menu brought the customers in by the hundreds. While the café was breaking even, it would take some time, possibly another year, to recoup the amount spent to expand the kitchen and serving area.

They were making the loan payments, but there were months when it was pretty tight and The Bastard knew it. The economy was slow and the bookstore's saving grace was that they sold both new and used books. Just in the past few months two other independent bookstores had gone under in New Orleans, and Holly was determined that Book Ends would not become number three.

The bottom line for her was that if the new lender chose to change the terms of her loan and increase the monthly payment, her store could be facing hard times. She sighed. One of the problems of owning your own business was that you never ceased to worry about it. And speaking of hard times, she had some bills to get out or the business phone and Internet access were in danger of being disconnected.

Holly reached into her in-box and picked up a pale gray envelope with her name written across the front in bold script. It was probably a party invitation, though she hadn't gone out since breaking up with The Bastard and most of her friends knew it.

She opened the envelope, then removed a single sheet of gray paper. Her gaze skimmed the letterhead and her heart stuttered. It was from the company that now held her loan.

Ms. Broussard,
I'd like to invite you to meet with me to discuss the new terms of your loan and possible payment options. Please join me on Thursday evening at seven o'clock at my office. If you have any questions or scheduling conflicts, please contact my secretary at the number above.

Sincerely,
E. Nathanial Clarke

Holly stared at the bold signature. Thursday, that was tomorrow.

Her gut tightened. "New terms" were enough to strike fear into any business owner's heart. Technically, a change in which bank held her loan should mean very little, as the lending companies were bound by state laws. As long as she made her payments on time and kept her credit clean there would be no issue. However, as far as she knew, the state could do nothing should this new company decide to increase the interest rate or payment amount.

He who held the mortgage made the rules.

Dropping the letter, she rose and walked to the railing of her loft office. It had originally been a warehouse; her parents had done most of the building renovations themselves from plastering the walls to refinishing the wood floor. Her stomach constricted as her gaze moved over the neat rows of shelves stuffed with thousands of books. Her father had built those shelves, and her mother had painted them while Holly had played at her feet.

A few customers milled about in the aisles, while others were seated in comfortable rocking chairs and overstuffed armchairs scattered throughout the store. Surrounded by stacks of books, two teenage girls were seated on the couch near the front windows, poring over fashion magazines with the intensity of a neurosurgeon.

Her heart swelled with pride. Even though she was biased, she thought Book Ends was a fantastic bookstore. They boasted a customer list in the tens of thousands and their author book signings were always well attended. The café was almost always packed and the phones rang incessantly.

Her business was a success.

For her, the best part was that many of her favorite childhood memories centered on this magical place. As a child she'd run up and down the aisles before collapsing in the children's book section, where she'd get lost in make-believe worlds where lions could speak and fauns really existed. Every Saturday, Holly hosted a children's reading hour and she wasn't sure who looked forward to it more, the kids or her.

The storeroom door opened and her junior partner, Katie, hurried out with a sheaf of plastic shopping bags over one arm. Her dark hair was its usual tumbled mess and Holly spied at least three pencils sticking out of the do.

Talking on the telephone, Melissa, her other junior partner, stood at the register. With her artfully tousled blondish-brown hair and trendy clothing, she was the picture of a fresh-faced college student. When Katie reached the desk, Melissa hung up the phone before she reached over and plucked two pencils from the other woman's hair. Both women started laughing and Holly couldn't help but smile.

These women depended upon her to keep Book Ends afloat. Katie was an only child who supported her ailing mother and her finances were always strained to the limit. Melissa was a single mother who was struggling to put herself through college to earn her business degree. Graduation would be a culmination of a lifelong dream, as she was the first person in her family to make it all the way through high school, let alone go to college.

Holly wrapped her arms around her waist as if to give herself a hug. Her parents were gone and these women were her family now. Book Ends was her legacy, her life, and she would do anything to protect it.

Two

Holly's nerves were in a knot by the time she walked through the gleaming doors of Clarke & Sons. The spacious lobby was understated with its muted grays and blues, and the marble floors gleamed. To her right was an impressive waterfall surrounded by lush foliage, and a circular reception desk was located in the center of the lobby between the doors and a bank of elevators. Two security guards were seated at the desk and one rose from his chair before he slipped on his suit jacket. She didn't miss the gun holster strapped under his left arm.

"Good evening, ma'am. How can I help you?" His smile was sharp, assessing, and she had no doubt that even if she never again set foot in this building, this man would remember her face.

"Holly Broussard, Mr. Clarke is expecting me." She offered him a bright smile that screamed "look how harmless I am," or so she hoped.

"Do you have some identification?"

Whoa, now this was some serious security.

Holly retrieved her driver's license from her purse and handed it to him. That sharp gaze focused on the slip of plastic, then returned to her face. "Nice to meet you, Ms. Broussard."

He handed her the license, then stepped out from behind the desk. "If you will follow me, ma'am."

Holly tucked her license into her purse, then fell into step behind the guard as he led her away from the main elevators toward another elevator door with no buttons, only a small flat red screen where they should have been located. He placed his hand over the screen and after a few seconds the panel flickered green and the door slid open.

"Here you are, Ms. Broussard. This elevator will take you directly to Mr. Clarke's office on the top floor." He moved to the side, his arm straight out to hold the door open. "Have a good evening, ma'am."

"Thank you." She stepped into the elevator and he moved away, allowing the door to slide shut.

The elevator rose, leaving her stomach on the first floor. Her grip tightened on her leather portfolio. This afternoon she'd spent several hours poking around on the Internet researching Clarke & Sons. With twin brothers, Ethan and Eric Clarke, at the helm, it was a family-owned firm specializing in import and real estate, though they'd recently purchased a popular restaurant chain. In the last year alone the company had grossed more than ten million in profits.

But why would they have purchased her loan? The amount due was less than one hundred thousand, not even a flyspeck in comparison to their ambitious business ventures. What would a multimillion-dollar company gain by purchasing her loan unless they wanted her to default so they could assume her commercial property?

The elevator stopped and the doors slid open. Squaring her shoulders, Holly stepped out into the lobby.

It was showtime.

* * *

Ethan Clarke stared hard at the closed-circuit television as Holly Broussard entered the outer office. Her expression was both curious and wary as she looked around his secretary's domain. Her flame-red hair was scraped back into a casual twist at the nape of her neck and her black suit was impeccably cut to her hourglass figure. Her heels were so high he marveled she could walk at all.

Without a doubt she was one of the most beautiful women he'd ever seen. He'd first been introduced to her at a bondage scene in the Quarter last year. Even though she'd been on the arm of Greg Mains, her brilliant red locks and mile-long legs had captivated Ethan. The moment their hands had touched he knew he had to claim her as his own, and soon he would.

In the monitor, his secretary, Gwen, ushered Holly toward a chair in the outer office. She sank into the leather chair, and when she crossed those spectacular legs, he thought his heart would stop.

He'd toyed with the idea of stealing her away from Mains. Knowing the man and his weaknesses, Ethan knew it wouldn't have taken much to accomplish his mission. But he'd learned Holly had left her Master after he'd violated her trust and beaten her, leaving her both scarred and mistrustful of men in general.

Ethan had bided his time, just barely managing to resist the urge to kill Mains with his bare hands. The bastard deserved a taste of his own medicine, a whipping like no other, but Ethan was a patient man. He knew sooner or later fate would deal Mains a crushing blow.

If it were up to him, it would be sooner.

When he'd learned Mains was intent on selling Holly's business loan to a national bookstore chain, Ethan had jumped on the chance to purchase it. Granted, he'd had to pay more than double the face value of the loan, but in his opinion she was more than worth it.

Holly hadn't been seen on the bondage scene since her breakup, and Ethan had it on good authority that she did little else but work and escape to her apartment over the bookstore. Even though his twin, Eric, had urged his brother to seduce Holly via the normal means, Ethan knew it wouldn't work with her. Through the grapevine he'd learned she'd made it clear to her friends she wasn't interested in pursuing a relationship with anyone right now. Whether this was a side effect of the broken relationship or the abuse she'd suffered, he wasn't sure, but he was determined to find out more about this woman.

Ethan switched off the monitor. Holly Broussard was the woman for him, she just didn't know it yet.

"Mr. Clarke." Holly held her hand out toward the man who now had control of her mortgage. He looked very familiar. Did he shop at her store?

"Please, call me Ethan." He took her hand in his and a jolt of awareness raced up her arm. His grip was firm, strong. "It is a pleasure to see you again, Ms. Broussard."

"Please, call me Holly." She tilted her head to the side. "Have we met before? Do you shop at the store?"

He shook his head. "I haven't had the pleasure of visiting Book Ends. We did meet though. Last year, I believe. It was at a social gathering in the Quarter." His smile was smooth, earthy, and her toes curled in the sheer pleasure of just looking at him.

"The Governor's Ball?"

"Ah, no. Nothing quite so auspicious, I'm afraid."

A particular glint in his eye alerted her to the fact he was probably referring to one of the bondage parties of which The Bastard had been so fond. Her stomach tightened. She'd always known at some point her after-hours activities would intrude upon her business life but it was too late to worry about it now. What's done was done.

"I hear you have an amazing bookstore," he continued. "I must make an attempt to pay you a visit sometime soon."

"Please do."

"Will you need me to stay, Mr. Clarke?" the sultry-voiced secretary said.

"No, thank you, Gwen. On your way home can you drop these at the post office?" With his focus on the stack of envelopes he was gathering together, Holly seized the opportunity to check him out.

He was tall, several inches taller than her own five-foot-ten and his muscular build fairly screamed *sex!* Dressed simply in dark slacks and a white dress shirt, he was a specimen to behold. His sleeves were rolled back to reveal tanned, muscular forearms liberally sprinkled with dark hair. His hair was black and neatly cut and styled, slightly longer on the top allowing a single lock to fall against his forehead. His features were even and his nose sported a slight bump as if it had been broken at some point. But it was his mouth that garnered most of her attention. It was generous and sensual, and if his face weren't quite so sharply hewn, it would have looked feminine. Holly felt curiously breathless just looking at him, a feeling she hadn't experienced in quite a while, not since well before The Bastard had entered her life.

"Please, have a seat." He flashed her a thigh-melting smile. "Can I get you a drink? Wine, perhaps?" He gestured toward a low-slung leather couch grouped with several comfortable-looking chairs.

"That would be lovely, thank you." Holly sank into a sumptuous armchair before opening her portfolio.

"I apologize for this last-minute meeting. This week has been very hectic and I wanted to talk to you about your loan and maybe set your mind at ease." He walked to a small refrigerator and removed a bottle of wine. "I'm sure you have quite a few questions."

"That I do. Obviously I'd like to go over the terms of the loan." She looked down at the list of questions she'd created earlier. "The current interest rate when the loan was held by—"

"The terms of the loan will not be changing." Ethan handed her a glass of white wine. "The interest rate, payment schedule, and finer points of the contract will remain as they were. My legal department is already drafting up a new contract and you should have it by the end of next week. Once everything is signed and notarized we can move on with our lives."

Startled, Holly set her glass on the table without tasting it. He wasn't changing the terms of the mortgage? So his company hadn't purchased the loan in an attempt to acquire her property? Then why had they gone through the trouble to purchase it in the first place? Something very strange was going on here.

"Mr. Clarke—"

"Ethan, please."

Holly smiled. "Ethan, I have to admit to being curious as to why your company decided to purchase the loan to begin with. The interest income is a mere pittance to a company the size of yours."

He shrugged. "There are several reasons why I made this move; the question is, are you ready to hear them?"

Her stomach began to churn. Just what the heck did he mean by that? "Of course I'm ready to hear the reasons, I did ask."

He gave her a slight smile. "My grandfather and his brothers created this company more than sixty years ago. They worked hard, put in long hours, and they loved every minute of it. Clarke & Sons is still a family-run business and it will remain that way. We understand the importance of heritage and we strive to preserve it.

"My cousin Niki Chaubert, who is a customer of yours, was researching some properties in the Quarter and she heard that Mains was beginning negotiations with one of those chain bookstores. It appears the chain was very interested in gaining control of your loan and ultimately your building. Niki felt this was an underhanded thing to do, so she called and gave me the details of your situation and here we are."

Holly blinked. The Bastard had been negotiating to sell her loan to one of the chains? Her hands fisted. He knew how she felt about those characterless chain stores, the most persistent of which she referred to as the Evil Empire. Considering his obvious animosity toward her it was the perfect move to make, as he knew it would have destroyed her business and broken her heart. She rubbed her hand over her stomach. Just the thought of someone hating her that much was enough to make her physically ill.

"Are you okay, Holly?" Ethan leaned forward. "Do you need a glass of water?"

"No, I think I need wine, lots of wine." Holly picked up her glass and took a healthy swallow.

"I realize some of this information is a bit of a shock to you. Chances are that Mains hadn't informed you he was negotiating to sell the loan. This is just my opinion but it seems he was quite intent upon selling the building out from under you."

Feeling steadier, Holly closed her portfolio and set it aside. "Why do you feel that way?"

"Mains was dead-set on selling to the chain. It took quite a bit of legal maneuvering and outbidding to remove them from the picture."

Holly's grip tightened on her glass. "Outbidding? You mean the mortgage wasn't purchased for the balance due?"

"No. My negotiator had to perform an elaborate dance to seal the deal and the price was considerably more than the amount due."

She took a deep, steadying breath. If the mortgage had been purchased for more than its current value, how much would that increase her monthly payment?

"Ethan, just how much was the mortgage purchased for?" Her voice was squeaky.

He named a figure that made her gulp.

"That much?" The urge to run across the room and chug the bottle of wine now sitting on the bar was almost irresistible.

His brow rose. "You don't think your business, your heritage, is worth that much money?"

She shook her head. "That isn't it at all. I can't put a price on what my business means to me. My reality is that in light of the recent expansions I simply can't afford to pay back that kind of money. We recently underwent some major renovations and for the next few months our cash flow is rather restricted—"

He held up his hand. "I've already told you the terms of your loan would not change, Holly. Your payments and everything else will remain the same."

"But the original loan won't cover this new amount. I cannot allow you to absorb the additional cost of the negotiated amount—"

"We have no intention of doing so, and I also realize you cannot possibly pay the amount we bought the loan for." He set his glass on the table. "This is why I'm prepared to make an unusual proposition. As I see it, we have two options on the table. You can agree to pay back the negotiated amount that Clarke & Sons paid out in order to acquire the loan, plus a modest interest rate. Once the loan is paid in full, the deed will be returned to you free and clear."

Holly's heart sank. There was no way she could pay that amount, not with the way the economy was headed. What would Katie and Melissa do if she let them down? What would she do if she lost the very roof over her head?

She had to clear her throat before she could speak. "And the second option?"

"The second option is a little more unusual. I am willing to write off the entire amount of the loan, more than a quarter of a million dollars, in exchange for a verbal agreement from you and three days of your time."

Her gaze narrowed. No company would be willing to undertake something this large unless it was illegal . . . or immoral. Her stomach cramped and she had a feeling she wasn't going to like the answer to the question, but she had to ask anyway.

"And what would that be?"

"Your agreement that you will become my lover for one weekend."

Three

SHE WANTED TO start screaming and never stop.

Holly stared at her computer screen, her back, shoulders, and neck ached from the long hours she'd sat hunched over her keyboard going through the store's financial records. She'd known even before she'd started this exhaustive review that the only way she could afford to pay the negotiated amount of the loan was to sell the business. The value of Book Ends as a business entity exceeded the loan amount by tens of thousands of dollars. On paper, she could sell the business and have more than enough to start over.

A sob caught in her throat.

Selling her heritage wasn't an option, as her pride wouldn't allow it. Her hands fisted. Over her dead body would she let The Bastard have the last word . . .

A burst of laughter from the store tore her attention away from her computer. It was a busy Friday morning and all of the tables in the café were filled to capacity. Melissa had a line of customers waiting to pay for their purchases while Katie and their part-time help, Serena, assisted those in the aisles.

This was all she'd ever wanted—to run the bookstore as her

parents had for so many years. She loved working with the stock for the sheer joy of holding a book in her hands. The thrill of discovering a new author or helping someone find a book they'd been searching for was immeasurable. She couldn't imagine doing anything else with her life.

As much as she needed to breathe or eat, she needed Book Ends.

Propped against her utilitarian telephone was the gray linen business card Ethan had given her last night. All she had to do was pick up the phone, make one call, and her future along with the employment future of her junior partners and employees would be secured. But what was she going to tell them? Katie and Melissa were more than just partners, they were her best friends and confidantes. How could she ever explain what she was about to do?

You can't . . .

She rubbed the tense spot between her eyes. The thought of having sex with a man, any man, made her half-sick to her stomach. Greg's abuse may have left physical scars, but the ones that couldn't be seen were far deeper and more paralyzing than the ones on her skin. She dropped her arm. She didn't know if she'd ever be able to trust enough to take a man into her bed anytime soon.

What choice do you have? Money doesn't grow on trees so unless you plan on winning the lottery next week . . .

She groaned. She had to be crazy to seriously entertain the idea of spending the weekend in bed with a complete stranger. She picked up the card.

It was funny but Ethan didn't *feel* like a stranger to her. According to him they'd met at a party though she didn't remember the incident. Oddly enough she'd felt at ease with him from the moment she'd entered his office, until he brought up the sex angle, that is.

She bit her lip, her gaze scanned the raised black letters. What kind of a man would want to have sex with a woman for a quarter of a million dollars? It was mind-boggling to say the least and she wasn't entirely sure she was up to the task. None of her previous lovers had ever had any complaints when it came to sex but that didn't mean she was worth *that* much money in the sack.

Why would a man as handsome as he even want to have sex with a woman at least five years his senior? Surely he could find his own women without having to buy her? Was he some kind of pervert, was that why he'd made her this offer? If he'd attended one of the party scenes, Ethan could be into any kind of kink. What if she ended up in the same position she'd found herself in with The Bastard?

Tied up . . .

Helpless . . .

Unable to defend herself . . .

She sighed.

Lying to herself would be pointless. She was reluctant to venture into a sexual relationship with anyone, let alone a complete stranger. Her relationship with The Bastard had turned into a nightmare and she'd never seen it coming. She'd trusted him implicitly and had ended up scarred both physically and mentally for her trouble. At this point she wasn't sure she could ever trust a man enough to have sex with him, let alone tie her up.

They'd had a Master-submissive relationship from the very beginning. The ultimate turn-on for her was the thrill of being restrained and submitting to a strong, dominant male. Not that she had anything against straight, vanilla sex—far from it. It was fine on certain occasions, but it was bondage and the concept that the sexual decisions were removed from her control and she was purely a vessel for pleasure. It was the only way she'd ever achieved multiple orgasms with a partner.

Ethan could be just like The Bastard . . .

It was very possible. Maybe he'd met her at a party and decided she was an anything-goes kind of woman and that was why he'd procured the loan in the first place. He'd also assured her that the decision regarding their loan arrangements was strictly up to her. She could either pay the astronomical amount of the note or submit to his less than businesslike proposal.

But could she have sex with a complete stranger?

She bit her lower lip. There was no doubt Ethan was hot, really hot. He was sexy, rich, intelligent, and straight. What more could a girl ask for?

Trust . . .

She sighed. Regardless of what she really wanted, Katie and Melissa were counting on her to secure the roof over their heads. Though she was reluctant, she was a practical woman who saw the writing on the wall.

Holly reached for the phone.

Ethan's attention was focused on his computer screen when the phone rang. Without shifting his gaze, he hit the speaker button.

"Yes?"

"Ms. Broussard called while you were out to lunch." Gwen's sexy voice floated out of the speaker. "She says she will accept your proposal."

He sat back and a rush of pleasure spread through his limbs to center in his groin. "Gwen, please contact her and make arrangements to send the car to her apartment at 7 p.m. this evening."

"Yes, sir. Is there anything else you need?"

"Not a thing. Thank you."

He hit the speaker button and disconnected. After all this time he could hardly believe it was true. The lovely Holly Broussard in his house, in his bed for three whole days. Ever since the night they'd met he'd dreamed of the moment he could stake his claim.

His blood heated at the thought of her coming to his bed. Yes, his methods were drastic and if his twin brother had any inkling of what he was doing he'd go through the roof. Ethan was personally going to have to eat a quarter of a million dollars just to pull this off, but that was superfluous in the face of being able to claim the woman who'd captivated his imagination for the past year. He had a feeling that she was *The One*.

The boxes had arrived just minutes before Holly was due to leave work. In a hurry to get her bags packed, she'd tucked them under her arm and dashed up the steps to her apartment over the store. She only had an hour before the car would be arriving and she still had a great deal to accomplish.

Laying the boxes on the kitchen table, she removed the top of the first one. A card lay on a bed of scarlet tissue paper and it read, *Looking forward to seeing you this evening, E*, in a black, masculine scrawl. A cool sweat broke out on her lip and she set aside the card. Opening the tissue paper, her eyes widened when she saw the blood-red roses. There were at least two dozen of them.

She trailed her fingers over the delicate blooms, marveling at their sheer beauty. The only time The Bastard had sent her flowers was after she'd broken off their relationship. Not once had he thought about sending them while they'd been together. What a jerk.

Holly set aside the flowers. The smaller box had the label of a high-end lingerie store on one corner. She removed the lid then opened the ivory tissue paper, her eyes widening when she saw the emerald green silk. It was a short chemise with delicate spaghetti straps and a saucy, fluted hem. The bodice was trimmed with tiny clear beads and accented with embroidery. Nestled beneath the garment was the matching thong.

Ethan definitely had class. This was quite an expensive gift for a temporary sex toy. Holly rubbed the silk between her fingers. This wasn't quite what she'd imagined when she'd agreed to this arrangement. She'd figured there would be very little seduction involved as, let's face it, the moment she'd picked up the phone she'd become a sure thing.

She dropped the silk. If she didn't know better she'd suspect he was trying to seduce her.

Four

Holly was convinced she was going to throw up in the middle of the living room. She pressed her damp palm against her stomach and said a silent prayer that she wouldn't disgrace herself. She'd arrived at Ethan's house just minutes ago to be greeted by a friendly woman who'd introduced herself as Ellen, the housekeeper. She'd led her here to await her host.

Looking down at the beautiful Oriental rug, Holly hoped vomit wouldn't ruin it. Rubbing a damp palm over her queasy stomach, she turned her attention to the room.

It was warm, cozy, with a fire in the large fireplace and walls lined with bookshelves stuffed to overflowing. The furniture looked comfortable, with an abundance of oversized pillows scattered about.

To calm her nerves, she drifted over to one of the shelves, her gaze automatically scanning the titles. It would appear that her host was very well read. The collection of recent bestsellers, classics, and technical manuals would make any bibliophile envious.

"Find anything interesting?"

Holly jumped when the deep masculine voice sounded behind her. She spun around, her cheeks going from ice-cold to blazing in seconds. Dressed in black from head to toe, Ethan stood in the doorway watching her.

"Occupational hazard." She nodded toward the shelves. "You have an impressive collection."

He walked into the room, his movements lazy, easy. "You could say that books are a passion of mine."

He was dressed casually in black jeans, a turtleneck, and suede moccasins. His dark hair, which had been perfectly styled in the office, was ruffled and a thick lock tumbled over his forehead giving him a boyish appeal. His blue eyes were sharp, intensely focused upon her, and she could almost feel the heat of his gaze. Without the suit and the neatly styled hair, he possessed a raw, edgy, sexy quality she hadn't picked up on during their meeting.

This man was more than hot, he was blazing.

She cleared her throat. "Um, yes. I could say the same thing. Books are a passion with me as well."

His smile was faint. "And in a way it is books that bring us together. You seek to save your store and I seek to save a New Orleans treasure." He gestured toward the bar. "Can I fix you something to drink?"

"Please." She sank into a chair before the fireplace. The heat from the fire was welcome. "My store means a great deal to me and I practically grew up in that building. After school I would go there and my mother would be waiting in the doorway every day. She spoiled me with chocolate chip cookies and free range of the shelves."

He walked toward her bearing two glasses of wine. "I can see why you would be so attached to it. Memories like that are a precious thing and they should be preserved if at all possible."

When he handed her the glass their fingers brushed, sending a bolt of electricity up her arm. Startled, she jerked away. His gaze sharpened and she knew he hadn't missed her reaction, but to her relief, he moved away without commenting.

"Holly, I admit I was a little surprised you accepted my offer." He picked up a fireplace poker and began rearranging the burning logs. "I know you recently left a relationship and that it ended badly for you. In light of that I would imagine you are a little reticent about this situation." The golden flames cast shadows over his sharp cheekbones giving him a vaguely Heathcliff-esque air.

She looked away, fixing her gaze on the pale gold of her wine. "You've done your homework."

"You expected any less from a copresident of a multimillion-dollar company?"

"No, I guess not." Normally Holly was a very private person but for some reason it didn't bother her that this man knew about her relationship with The Bastard. "And what did you learn about me?" She took a sip from her glass, enjoying the crisp flavor of the ice-cold chardonnay.

"That you dated Greg Mains for approximately a year and you left him when his play became too rough."

Their gazes met and she gave him a slight nod. "Well, you are thorough."

His lips tightened. "I'm very sorry that happened to you as you deserve so much better. A Master's first and most important responsibility is the safety and welfare of his submissive, not his own lust."

Holly's gaze danced away. "I can't argue with you there."

"I give you my word that won't occur between us. I promise

you when you're with me you will be safe as you'll call the shots." He gave her a slight smile. "In bed at least."

Her gut tightened. "So, you expect a Master-submissive relationship with me. This weekend."

"I have no expectations here, Holly. I understand that you would be reluctant to enter into this type of relationship with a man you know, let alone a complete stranger." He replaced the poker. "However, I would like the opportunity to remind you what a Master, a real Master, can do for his lover."

Judging from the seriousness of his expression, Ethan believed everything he was telling her. But did she believe him? Could she trust this man with both her mind and her body?

She took another sip of her wine, allowing the tension to build before she spoke. "And what if I say no to that arrangement?"

"Then we negotiate."

She blinked. This wasn't quite what she'd expected. She was grateful that Ethan was being up front with her and she did appreciate that aspect of his personality. While Holly couldn't deny her desire to learn more about this man, she also wouldn't deny the fear she held in her heart. Right now both emotions weighed heavily upon her.

"How about this as an added incentive?" Ethan walked over to his desk and picked up a beige folder. "Here are the loan papers along with the deed to the property which you'd put up for collateral. I will hand these over to you this evening, no questions asked, if you agree to a submissive-Master relationship."

Shocked, all Holly could do was stare at him for a moment. He would do that? Just let her walk away with no questions asked? Was this man totally insane?

"I want you to walk into this arrangement knowing that if at any time you feel uncomfortable or that I have abused our relationship, you are free to leave and your debt will be erased."

"If I get uncomfortable I can just walk away?" Doubt laced her words. "You would eat a quarter of a million dollars, just like that?"

"In these circumstances, yes I would." He walked toward her with the folder in his hand. "I want you to trust me and if it takes handing you the keys to securing your future then so be it."

The folder was so tantalizingly close, her financial freedom and the future of her business was within her grasp. She reached for it, surprised to see that her hand was shaking. Opening the folder, her gaze skimmed over the papers. It was as he'd said, the deed to her property was in the folder along with the release paperwork. Little cellophane arrows pointed to the lines where her signature was needed. Ethan's end was already taken care of.

She closed the folder. He was showing her that he trusted her to carry out her end of the bargain, now the question was, could she afford to grant him the same amount of trust?

With her gaze fixed on the folder, she laid it in her lap, her folded hands resting on top. "And you'll listen to me when and if I tell you to stop?" The words came from a distance as if it were someone else who was speaking.

"Without hesitation."

Her body felt cold and shaky while her palms grew moist. Even though she was hesitant, she realized that she wanted this badly. For once and for all she needed to rid herself of the fear hanging over her head that The Bastard had inflicted upon her. To feel a man's hands on her body once more, to submit her sensual side to a man's pleasure thus securing her own, and knowing all the while she was safe with him, would go a long way to healing her scarred psyche, and Ethan was just the man to help her.

"Only for this weekend." Her lips felt oddly numb as she spoke.

"If that is your wish."

Did he hesitate before answering? Their gazes met. "That is what I wish. This relationship will go no further than Sunday evening and after that you will make no attempt to call or pressure me in any way."

His brow arched. "I see you've thought about this."

She shook her head. "I just want to ensure we're on the same page before we begin. I don't want anything but complete honesty and understanding between us."

He raised his glass. "As you wish."

She swallowed hard. "Okay, it's a deal." Her voice was faint.

"You won't regret this, Holly." He reached for her, taking her hand. "This will be a mutually satisfying experience for both of us."

Her skin tingled where his fingers touched hers. Ethan raised her hand to his mouth and her breath left in a rush when his lips touched her knuckles. Her knees felt liquid and her body went warm, damp.

"What would you like your safe word to be, Holly?" he whispered against her skin.

"M-my middle name, Eleanor."

"Lovely name." He stepped back, pulling her with him. "Come, let's head upstairs and make ourselves more comfortable."

Like a security blanket, Holly tucked the folder under her arm. With her hand nestled in the crook of his arm, she walked beside him on wobbly legs. He led her up a wide staircase and into the upper hall. The floors were covered in heavy canvas drop cloths, and scaffolds lined one wall.

"Please excuse the mess, the ceilings are being redone up here. The spring rains really did a number on the ceiling as the roof sprang a few small leaks. Nothing like owning a house that is several hundred years old, something is always falling apart."

Holly smiled. "I am familiar with the syndrome. It seems like I'm constantly repairing my building as well."

"And you live above the store?"

"I do. When I took over the business I converted part of the loft area into an apartment for myself. Saved on commuting time."

He chuckled. "I'll bet." Ethan led her through a set of double doors and into a small sitting room. "This is the master suite. Your room is to the right and mine is here on the left." He pointed to each door.

Startled, Holly looked up at him. "We aren't sharing a room?"

"I'm leaving that decision totally up to you." His expression was enigmatic. "If you feel comfortable in doing so, I would love to have you in my bed for the entire time you're under my roof. If you don't feel comfortable in doing that then you can retreat to your room for some privacy and quiet time."

Touched, she had to clear her throat before she could respond. "Thank you, I appreciate that."

She slipped her hand from his arm and walked toward the fireplace where a fire was already warming the room. A chaise lounge and a wing chair were situated before the crackling fire, and between them was a coffee table with a tray covered with a silk scarf.

"Have you much experience as a Master?" She took a gulp of her wine to steady her nerves. She perched on the edge of the wing chair, the folder clutched in one hand and her wineglass in the other.

"Quite." He stretched out on the chaise looking every inch the master of the house, crossing his legs at the ankle. "I've had three long-term submissives and several other casual relationships."

"And what happened with your last submissive?" She placed her precious folder on the floor next to her chair, reluctant to release it but knowing that her death grip on it was doing nothing to loosen her nerves.

"The lady fell in love with my best friend." He shrugged. "We weren't in love and I'm the last person to stand in the way of another's happiness. I threw his bachelor party last year and they're expecting their first child in September."

"That was very nice of you."

"It was the least I could do." He smiled. "It seems to me that, as your Master, I should be the one asking you the questions."

"Go ahead."

"What turns you on sexually?"

Holly almost choked on her wine.

"Are you okay?" he asked.

She nodded and took a few seconds to regain her breath. "Well, that was direct."

He shrugged. "That's how I like to live my life. Life is too short to dance around intimate topics and I prefer to tackle issues head-on."

She nodded. "As do I."

"Besides, how can I please you if I don't know what you enjoy in bed?" He sipped his wine. "Do you enjoy being bound?"

Her cheeks warmed and she squirmed in her chair. "Very much."

"Spanked?"

"Yes." Her nipples beaded, the soft lace of her bra chafed the tender tips.

"How about anal sex?"

A strong rush of liquid warmth ran through her body and she didn't trust her voice, so instead of speaking she nodded before tossing back the remains of her wine.

"This pleases me very much." Ethan finished his wine before setting the glass aside. He crossed his arms over his stomach, his gaze intent upon her. "Please remove your panties, Holly."

After years of being a submissive, it never occurred to her to not do as he bid. Rising from the chair, she pulled up her skirt to shimmy the emerald green thong down her legs. Stepping out of them, she left them lying on the carpet.

His look was approving. "Very nice. You may sit down."

Holly sat and primly crossed her legs, wondering if the flesh between her legs was wetter than her slick palms. Arousal and nervousness warred in her stomach and she regretted chugging the last of her wine.

"While you're in my home you'll be forbidden to wear panties. I enjoy knowing that my woman is bare beneath her clothing. It excites me.

"Now, I want you to touch yourself while I watch." He leaned forward to remove the silk scarf from the tray to reveal an array of sexual devices. There were dildos of varying sizes in materials from glass to latex to hard plastic. Several vibrators along with butt plugs of varying sizes were lined up beside a fresh tube of lubricant.

Her mind screamed for her to run from this situation even as her body went liquid and her sex grew wet. Arousal was winning the battle against her nervousness. Slowly, she spread her legs, draping one over the arm of the chair. Shifting forward, her hips rested on the edge of the chair, facing Ethan.

Just those few, nonthreatening movements had her sex weeping for release. Just the feel of his hot gaze moving over her body and she was ready to come. Blowing out a long breath, she steadied herself before pulling up her skirt to bare her sex to his gaze. She knew what he'd see as she'd had a Brazilian bikini wax only a week ago leaving her mound nearly bare with only a strip of silky red curls.

At the first touch of her fingers, she sighed and pressed her hips harder against the chair. Moving deeper, she began stroking her clit, sending lightning bolts of sensual excess through her body. She stroked her clit and her vagina clenched, desperate for something, anything to penetrate her. With her free hand she reached between her thighs and entered herself with a finger. A soft moan escaped her when her vagina clamped down as if to draw it deeper.

Adding a second finger, her hips bucked against the increased sensation and a soft whimper broke from her throat. After a few strokes she knew it felt good but it just wasn't quite enough to give her the release she craved.

Removing her fingers, she sat up and inspected the toys on the tray before choosing a sleek, glass dildo. In the depths of the glass, colored strands swirled, red, purple, and gold in the firelight. The cool glass would feel like heaven against her heated flesh. She took a small amount of the lubricant and began oiling up the smooth glass, all the while very aware of the man sitting across from her. Once it was slick, she leaned back in her seat.

Spreading her pussy wide, she settled the cold glass against her vagina and pushed. She moaned as the dildo stretched her flesh as it penetrated her, teasing the nerve endings into awareness. It was smaller than most men's cocks she'd experienced but it had been so long, too long since she'd taken a man into her body it felt like she was a virgin all over again. Her inner muscles contracted and she squirmed against the icy invasion of her glass lover. It was hard, impossibly hard and it stretched her just enough to jolt her body into responsiveness. Grasping the base, she began to ride the glass cock.

What would it be like to be possessed by the man watching her? Was he a tender, thoughtful Master or did he enjoy the darker, more dangerous side of the bondage scene? Her gaze moved to his groin where his hardened cock pressed against his jeans. Judging from the size of the bulge, Ethan Clarke was a big man among men. Her gaze met his and she licked her lips.

Very aware of his hot, dark gaze upon her, she leaned her head back and closed her eyes. Working her glass lover in and out of her pussy she began the climb to release. Stroking her clit with her free hand, her breathing grew ragged and her body begged for release. With every thrust, her greedy cunt, thrilled at being relieved of its forced celibacy, sucked at the dildo. Her inner muscles clamped down even as her back arched. A cry broke from her mouth as shudders racked her body.

five

Holly tilted her head and allowed the hot water from the showerhead to rinse the shampoo from her hair. She felt . . . good. No, more than good.

She felt empowered.

Having Ethan play the voyeur as she'd pleasured herself had been liberating in a way that was difficult to contemplate. It was as if with the simple act of taking satisfaction in her body's responses, she'd reclaimed something that had been stolen from her. When The Bastard had taken away her choice by ignoring her use of the safe word, he'd not only damaged her trust in her own judgment, he'd also destroyed her faith in men.

In handing her the loan papers and deed to her property, Ethan had earned her trust and ultimately granted her a complete sense of freedom. Though Holly realized she wasn't healed, for the first time in many months she felt as if the darkness had been dispelled, if only a little bit. She was truly alive and well on her way to moving on with her life.

Holly hugged the knowledge to her heart as she finished rinsing her hair. Her mama had always maintained that the best revenge was gained by living well, and wouldn't it burn The

Bastard's butt to know that she was doing so much better emotionally—

She heard a clatter in the bathroom just before the door to the oversized shower cubicle opened. She gasped and spun around, looking for something with which to cover herself, but she only had a washcloth and a bar of soap.

Ethan stood in the doorway, his heated gaze moving over her damp, soapy flesh. "You're very beautiful."

She shivered. "Thank you." With him she felt beautiful for the first time in a long while. She dropped the washcloth.

"How do you feel about water sports?" A glint entered his eye that ignited a slow buzz of heat in her blood. Ethan reached for his belt buckle to release it before opening the front of his jeans. She swallowed hard, her insides going liquid-soft when he removed his turtleneck to reveal a hard, sculpted, masculine chest. He wasn't a bodybuilder but he was strong, sturdy, and well-defined. Muscles rippled across his chest and belly and her fingers ached to explore their terrain.

"I feel . . . wet," she whispered.

"Mission accomplished."

She licked her dry lips when he removed the rest of his clothing. Jutting proudly from a thatch of black hair, his cock was a thing of beauty. Long and thick, it begged for the caress of her tongue. He stepped into the shower with her and her breathing grew shallow.

"I want you very badly, Holly." He stood near her, water sluicing over their bodies so close yet so far apart. "I want to touch every inch of you, with my hands." He skimmed his fingers over her shoulder then the plump curve of her breast. She whimpered when he thumbed her nipple. "With my mouth."

Oh my God . . .

He leaned forward and brushed his lips against her jaw. "I want to taste you as you come against my mouth."

Her knees began to shake and she put her hands on his shoulders for balance.

"Kiss me," she whispered.

"With pleasure."

With her back against the slick wall of the shower and his big, hard body pressing into her, his head dipped low. His mouth was hard against hers, strong and possessive as his tongue touched hers. She moaned deep in her throat when he began sucking at her flesh.

Her nails dug into his shoulder before he removed them. Pulling her arms over her head, he pinned her to the wall with one hand. A wave of arousal slammed through her body when he pressed into her, completing the illusion of her helplessness in the face of his need. He kissed his way down her throat and she arched to give him better access. The scent of his aftershave mixed with hot, male arousal and soap, was causing her to melt both inside and out.

"You're so sweet." He licked the hollow of her throat. "Hot."

Her breathing hitched and he leaned into her, crowding her against the wall. Her nipples tightened and they ached to be touched. She barely resisted the urge to rub against him like a cat in heat. The flesh between her thighs ached even though only minutes before she'd experienced a mind-blowing orgasm in the sitting room.

He bit her shoulder and the resulting rush of arousal told her once would never be enough with this man.

"I want you to touch me," he gritted out. His eyes were dark with heat and his jaw was hard. He released his grip on her wrists and guided her hands to his cock where it was nestled against her belly. He pulled back slightly to give her room to move, his hands coming to rest on her hips.

Her fingers curled around his cock and he moaned when she gave him a gentle squeeze. He was as hard as steel and hot as the late afternoon sun. She ran her thumbs over the broad tip and he shuddered. She pressed closer and rubbed her nipples against his chest and his groan almost sent her over the edge. Cupping his balls, she moved against him like a cat, dragging her nipples against his chest. The sensations made her head spin. Even though it had been a long time since she'd had a man, she was sure she'd never experienced something quite this primal.

He took her by the waist then lifted her until her breasts were level with his mouth. She wrapped her legs around him like a vine and braced her hands on his shoulders. He caught one hardened bud and gave it a firm suckle. Her head fell back and she cried out as sensation zinged from her breasts down to her mound in one fell swoop.

"Brace yourself, I'm coming inside you," he gritted out.

Her mind melted at the erotic image. He then worked his arms under her legs and grabbed her ass, holding her in place. He pressed her knees up toward her chest and with her legs over his arms it left her spread and vulnerable.

"You're mine, Holly."

He entered her with a slow thrust that stole her breath. Her body stretched to envelop him and when he began to thrust, the friction was incredible. The position he'd arranged gave her no defenses against him. His thick cock worked her flesh, his thrusts deep and rhythmic and she took every one, all the while begging for more.

Tension curled just below the skin then spun wildly out of control. She felt her climax coalesce low in her belly as his cock stroked her clit with each thrust. Her nails dug into his shoulders and he vaulted her over the edge. Stars sparked against her eyelids as her release tore through her body.

She arched her back and let loose with a wild scream of completion then promptly burst into tears.

"I'm sorry." Her words were muffled against the thick collar of her bathrobe.

"I'm not." Still nude, Ethan scooped her up in his arms and carried her into the bedroom. She smelled good, of soap and warm female flesh. "You obviously needed to cry or it wouldn't have happened."

"Talk about lousy timing," she sniffed.

He chuckled. "No, lousy timing would have been about thirty seconds earlier." He set her on the edge of the bed. "That might have deflated my . . ." he looked down at his cock, ". . . ego."

Giggling, she slipped under the covers. "Somehow I doubt that."

"You think?" He moved around the room and turned off the lights. "It could happen." Climbing into bed with her, he was gratified when she immediately snuggled against him.

"When did we meet? What party was it?"

"It was Vance's annual Halloween party." He slid his arm around her shoulders and rested his cheek against her fragrant head. "You were dressed as a harem girl in emerald green and sapphire blue."

"That was a while back." She yawned. "You remembered me after all that time?"

It was on the tip of his tongue to say that a man always remembered the moment he fell in love, but he couldn't say it, not yet.

"That dress of yours didn't leave a great deal to the imagination. I always remember a great rack."

"You're such a *guy*." She gave a sleepy laugh and her arm snaked across his stomach. "Lucky me."

"Go to sleep, slave. I have plans for you later."

She gave a sleepy purr, then snuggled closer. Within moments she'd fallen asleep.

Ethan lay in the darkness, his arm around Holly, their bodies separated by her thick terrycloth robe. He hadn't been kidding when he'd said her dress hadn't left much to the imagination. For months, the thought of her nubile body wrapped in that sheer green material had been enough to give him a king-sized erection. Nothing, nothing in his wildest imagination had prepared him for the reality of having Holly in his arms. His fantasies hadn't even come close to how making love to the woman had been.

Magical.

He ran his fingers over the curve of her shoulder. When he'd heard what Mains had done to her, it had taken all of his restraint to prevent himself from tracking the bastard down and throttling him where he stood. No woman should ever be hurt by a man, and certainly not his woman.

Ethan kissed her forehead and inhaled the soft, floral fragrance of her hair. His eyes slid closed, contentment flooded his body. He had her exactly where he wanted her, now he just needed to deal a crushing blow of retribution to Greg Mains.

Six

"It's time."

Rubbing her eyes, Holly rolled onto her back. The sheets were tangled beneath her and her body resonated with a lovely sense of bonelessness that came from having really excellent sex. She shoved her tumbled hair out of her eyes.

Dressed in black sweatpants and nothing else, Ethan towered over the bed. His hair was sleep-tousled and he looked sexy in a rumpled, I-just-got-out-of-bed-after-having-wild-sex kind of way.

Yummy. Just the way she liked her men.

"What is it time for?" She glanced at the clock, her eyes widening when she saw the time. "It's only 2 a.m., it's time to sleep."

"On the contrary, it's time to play."

The playful, sensual gleam in his eyes ignited an answering heat in her body. Slipping from the bed she snagged a T-shirt from her bag before falling into step behind him. Ethan waited for her to put on some slippers before he led her the short distance down the hallway to a door at the end. Opening the door, he stepped aside to allow her to enter first.

It was pitch-black and the scent of vanilla and leather teased her senses. He hit the wall switch and muted lighting flooded the room, causing her to blink. When her eyes adjusted, her breath caught as she took in the chamber of delights he'd led her to.

Erotic artwork depicting various sexual acts with bondage and discipline being the predominant theme adorned the ivory walls. An impressive selection of whips, paddles, and blindfolds along with some devices she'd never seen before were neatly arranged in a mahogany armoire on the far wall. A padded massage table with leather restraints was situated next to it along with something that looked like a padded sawhorse. In the opposite corner was an ornate wrought-iron cage large enough to contain a full-sized adult. In the center of the room, a sling was hung from the ceiling and around it there were several leather couches.

"Come." Ethan took her hand and led her to a massage table, her feet sinking into the plush red carpeting. "I think you will find this to your liking." The table was equipped with leather restraint devices for the hands and feet. At the sight of the straps, her body went cold.

"I'm not sure I'm ready." Her voice came out a little wobbly.

"Holly, you don't have to be afraid." He raised her hand and touched her knuckles with his mouth. "We won't do anything you aren't ready for." He released her hand then picked up one of the wrist restraints. "These are probably a little different than what you've used before now. Instead of being secured with a buckle this one has a pin." He slipped the restraint around his own wrist and slid the metal pin into place to secure it. "You can release this type of restraint without my assistance and this leaves you in total control of what happens."

Control.

Ethan removed the cuff with his bound hand then allowed Holly to inspect it. She slipped on the cuff and saw that she could easily release herself with the same hand. Ingenious. There was no way he could keep her prisoner with a design such as this. With her heart in her throat she gave him a tentative nod.

"That's my girl."

Holly removed her T-shirt then allowed Ethan to help her onto the table. The padded leather was cool beneath her buttocks and she shivered.

"It will warm up soon enough." He kissed the inside of her wrists as he secured each one. When he moved to fasten a restraint to one of her legs, he skimmed his hand down the inside of her thigh. "You're an exquisite submissive, Holly." He slipped the restraint around her ankle. "More so than I'd ever dared to dream."

"Dream?" She checked to see that she could still reach the release pins on her wrists before giving the restraints a tentative tug. "Why on earth would you be dreaming of me?"

He gave her a wicked grin. "I'm telling you, it was that green dress of yours." He kissed her knee, sending a jolt of sensation dancing along her nerves. "It has haunted me."

She laughed. "I still have it at home if you want me to bust it out for you."

He gave her a mock leer. "Now, that's what I'm talking about. That dress and a pair of high heels—what more could a man desire from his woman?"

She laughed and he picked up her other leg. Giving it the same treatment, he teased and caressed her flesh until she was bound to the table with her thighs splayed wide.

"You're utterly responsive." Her vagina clenched when she felt the gentle brush of his fingertips against the narrow strip of pubic hair. "Are you comfortable?"

She flexed her shoulders. "Yes, Master."

"Very good, my pet. It is very important for you to understand that in my domain, you must ask permission for release." He trailed his fingers over the soft swell of her belly then between her breasts. His eyes were hot with sensual promise. "You must not come without my permission and, just because you ask, doesn't necessarily mean that you shall receive." He swirled his finger around one erect nipple. "Do you understand?"

"Yes." Her voice came out as a hiss. When he plucked the hardened bead, her vagina clenched. While an edge of doubt lingered in the back of her mind, arousal was quickly overshadowing what few fears she harbored about being vulnerable to this man.

"Do you know what really turns me on?" he asked.

Her tongue felt thick and she didn't trust herself to make a coherent sentence so she opted to shake her head.

"Seeing you, like this." He touched her nipple, a faint caress that earned a sound of protest from her when he moved away. "Your hair spread out on the table, your body so open to me and ready to slake my desires. You're so beautiful, I almost forget how to breathe."

He bent and covered her nipple with his mouth, suckling one then the other. A sigh escaped her and she allowed her eyes to close as she gave herself over to his masterful mouth. In a silent invitation she arched her back, pressing her buttocks into the soft leather.

He moved his hand between her thighs as he sucked harder

on her nipple. Stroking the inside of her thigh, he released her nipple to trace a damp path of fire over her abdomen with his tongue, pausing only to nip at her belly button. He stroked his fingers over her pussy and she gave a low moan.

"Soon I will be inside you again," he spoke against her lower belly.

"Yes, Master—"

Her words were cut off when he entered her with one finger. Twisting against her restraints, she was both delighted and dismayed to find that they held her almost immobile. Her fists knotted as he began to finger-fuck her.

"Your pussy is so sweet." His voice was strained. "I want to sink my cock into you. I want to make you come beneath me until thoughts of any other man having you are obliterated from your memory."

At the first heated lap of his tongue over her clit, her hips arched as far as the restraints would allow. She moaned and tried to spread her thighs even farther to invite him in but the restraints held her in place. Never had she been so aroused yet frustrated at the same time.

"My God, but you're the perfect submissive and I have to have you," he muttered. Stripping out of his sweatpants, he climbed onto the table between her thighs.

"Hurry," she panted.

She sucked in a harsh breath when he lowered his body over hers, and the broad head of his cock brushed the opening of her aching pussy. With his arms braced on either side of her body, his eyes were closed as he entered her inch by slow inch. His expression was dreamy and he pulled back slightly, before pushing in further until he was buried to the hilt. He pulled out then entered her again with a slow, rolling thrust. His cock hit her sweet spot and she gave a long, low moan, needing something yet not quite sure what she wanted other than release.

"Please, Master. Harder," she whispered.

He picked up the pace, thrusting in and out in deep, even strokes. The table squeaked in unison to his movements and Holly lost herself in his effortless sensuality. Arousal shimmered over her flesh in arcs of light and soon she was beyond coherent thought other than the need for release.

"More, please Master," she panted.

He looked down at her, his expression strained yet tender. "Greedy wench. I think you forget who is in charge here."

He stopped thrusting and pulled out completely. She opened her mouth to protest until she felt him release her from the ankle restraints. Overjoyed that she could move, Holly wrapped her legs around his waist after he entered her again with a slow thrust. She gave an earthy moan as he began hammering into her, back and forth in fast, deep movements, each one stroking her clit at just the right angle. His expression grew hard, perspiration dotted his brow, and his eyes darkened as he fucked her into mindless, animal awareness of him.

Her eyes slid shut as the pressure built low and hard in her belly, her pussy, and thighs. She was unable to do anything other than feel what he gave her, the incredible pleasure his body brought to hers. Without warning her orgasm broke over her like the sea against the rocks. Lightning streaks blinded her closed eyes and she came around him in a wave of pleasure.

Slowly reality reasserted itself and she opened her eyes. His upper body was braced on his arms, his expression was dark, sensual. A slow smile curved his handsome sculpted mouth.

"It looks like a punishment is in order. You didn't ask permission for release, my beautiful slave."

Holly sat on her heels in the center of the bed staring at her lover. "You want me to do what?"

Ethan stretched his arms behind his head, his posture one of complete relaxation. He was nude, his big body sprawled in the midst of the rumpled sheets, and she was struck by the urge to lick him from head to toe.

Too bad he was intent upon spanking her right now.

"You disobeyed a direct order from your Master and now, you must take your punishment. We'll begin once you present yourself to me."

She cocked her head. "What do you mean by that?"

"Lay across my knees so that I can see your beautiful ass."

Her stomach quivered and her indecision must have shown on her face.

"Holly, what is your safe word?"

"E-Eleanor."

"Good girl. Do you wish to use it now?"

She licked her dry lips, her heart thundered in her chest. She shook her head then slowly crawled across the bed. Lying facedown across his thighs, she balanced her chin on her crossed arms on the edge of the bed and tried to relax.

"That's better."

His warm hands landed on the small of her back before following the curve of her rump. She tensed when they reached the thin scar that marred her buttocks. He said nothing, only shifting forward until she felt the tender touch of his mouth on the narrow mark.

"He should be flayed alive for this." Ethan's voice was little more than a rage-filled whisper.

Tears stung her eyes and she blinked to prevent them from falling. "Trust me, karma will deal with The Bastard in its own leisurely time."

"With a little help it can be sooner rather than later."

She chuckled. "He really isn't worth the effort. Revenge is a bitter dish that will only serve to lower me to his standards should I give in to it."

He nipped at the curve of her buttock, eliciting a squeak from her. "You're a smart woman, Holly."

She grinned. "I'd like to think so."

His big hands resumed their leisurely stroking. "I don't relish punishing you, my pet."

His impressive erection pressed into her hip, belied his words. She gave a silky squirm, deliberately pressing into his cock. "Somehow I doubt that."

"Hush, my impudent slave." He gave her a gentle slap on the butt. "You must understand who the Master is in this relationship. It is I who give you the commands and you who must obey them." He began to rub her buttocks and upper thighs in long, sensual strokes. "I want you to be nothing less than totally willing when you come to me, Holly."

Need streaked through her body when he nudged her thighs apart leaving her exposed. The air was cool against her damp flesh. She squirmed, helpless and needy, so very needy.

"Yes, Master."

He gave her a gentle spank on one buttock, then the other.

Her flesh heated and she squirmed with pleasure. Her back arched, pushing her buttocks even higher and her eyes drifted shut and she gave a soft purr . . .

His hand came down again, only this time it wasn't quite so gentle. She gave a startled squeal and her head came up off her crossed arms. Warmth blossomed across her buttocks as the blows rained down, some lighter, some heavier and all were arousing.

The sound of his hand against her buttocks mingled with their harsh breathing and her occasional groans. Fire spread across her buttocks as he spread the punishment around, taking care that no two slaps landed in the same place. With each stroke her hips followed the movement until she struggled to find something to relieve the unending arousal at the apex of her thighs.

"Your ass is a beautiful shade of pale pink, Holly." He sounded breathless.

The blows had slowed but each one was more painful, thanks to the previous ones. She spread her thighs in an effort to relieve some of the discomfort.

"Are you sorry you disobeyed your Master, Holly?"

"Yes," she panted.

The blows stopped.

"Are you wet for me?" he whispered.

Unable to speak, she nodded. A sharp slap landed across her ass and her cunt tightened even as liquid arousal flooded her vagina.

"You will speak when I ask you a question."

"Yes, I'm wet for you," she sobbed.

His hand came down for one last swat and she screamed. Before the pain faded he slid his hand between her thighs and parted her flesh. She moaned as his fingers brushed her clit.

"Come for me, now."

She was helpless in the face of her dark desire and his masterful touch. It took only a few swift strokes to bring her to climax. Her nails dug into the sheets as heat raced along her spine and she came against his hand.

Ethan disconnected his cell phone and laid it on the desk. In light of recent events he couldn't help but feel victorious. He had the woman of his dreams waiting for him upstairs and the man who'd dared to hurt her would be broken in half within the next two days.

He exited the library and headed for the steps. In reality it hadn't taken much to find dirt on Greg Mains. While his brother Doug was as clean as a choirboy, it would seem that Greg had a taste for cocaine and embezzlement. And all it had taken was one well-paid private detective with a head for numbers and a long-range camera lens. Within hours, copies of incriminating photographs and supporting documentation would be on their way to the largest television stations and newspapers in New Orleans. Once they were made public, the demise of Greg Mains would be complete.

Life didn't get any better than this.

He shut the sitting room door behind him then headed for the bedroom, shedding his robe as he moved. Holly lay in the middle of the bed where he'd left her. Early morning sunlight illuminated the lush curves of her ass causing his mouth to water. Only a few hours before they'd had explosive, mind-blowing sex in the dungeon and already he wanted her again. He climbed onto the bed, his movements causing her to stir.

"Ethan?" Her voice was sleepy-soft.

"Yeah, babe." He covered her, settling his body over hers.

"Just making sure it's you," she purred.

He chuckled and nuzzled the curve of her shoulder. Her plump backside cradled his cock and he braced his arms on his elbows to prevent crushing her. She was made for lovemaking, her body was lush and womanly and the noises she made when she was aroused were music to his ears. Much to his gratification she was wildly responsive to every little touch, caress. His teeth grazed the tender skin at the base of her neck eliciting a purr from her mouth. Now he'd have to see how responsive she was to his next command.

"Holly, have you ever been fucked in the ass?"

She lifted her head from the pillows, her hair a tangled halo of fire. "Oh, yes." She looked over her shoulder at him and gave him a wicked smile. "Did you know the anus has more nerve endings than the vagina?"

"No I didn't. I think this might be something I'll need to investigate further."

"Mmm, so I get to fuck you in the ass?" Amusement laced her words.

Ethan laughed. "I don't think so." He rose and reached for a tube of lubricant from the bedside table.

"What are you doing?"

"I'm getting ready to fuck you in the ass."

Beneath him her hips gave a silky shimmy. "Shall I assume the position?" She sounded breathless, aroused.

"On your knees, slave, prepare to be taken by your Master."

Holly flashed him an excited grin and together they gathered the pillows and made a mound in the center of the bed. When they were done she stretched out, her hips on the top of the mound and her body draped on each side, her head resting on her crossed arms.

"Are you comfortable?" He patted her on the ass.

"Mmm, very."

"Good." He parted her thighs, spreading them wide until her glistening cunt and puckered ass were exposed. He couldn't resist tasting her, his tongue zeroing in on her slick clit. She made a breathy sound, her back arching to give him better access. He pulled away. "Patience."

She groaned.

Ethan removed the top from the tube. "This will probably be a little cool. I'm going to squirt some lubricant in your ass."

"Use a lot, please."

"I will. I don't wish to hurt you." He slipped his hand between her thighs, sliding one finger into her cunt. "You're very wet, Holly. I see the thought of my taking you from behind has you aroused."

He began stroking her, his fingers sliding in and out of her wet flesh. She moaned and her hips picked up his rhythm. Slipping the narrow mouth of the lubricant tube into her anus, he gave it a healthy squeeze. The sound of her fingernails digging into the sheets caused his hair to stand on end.

"How are you feeling?" he asked.

"Hot."

"I'm going to enter you with my finger." He applied more lubricant to her anus, taking time to spread it around before attempting to enter her. He pressed his finger against the tight ring of protective muscle until she relaxed and let him inside.

"More." She squirmed, her anus tightening around him.

"As you command." He chuckled and added a second finger

to spread the lubricant across her needy flesh. "Feel good?" He leaned forward and kissed the base of her spine.

"Oh, yes."

She was ready.

Ethan slipped his fingers out of her anus then rose onto his knees. "I'm coming inside, Holly."

He pressed his cock against her glossy ass, pressing back and forth until her hips began to follow the movement. Sliding his slick hand over his cock, he lubed up until it glistened with slickness. He grasped her by the hips and positioned himself against her tight opening.

"Relax, baby."

He reached around and began to massage her clit until she sighed with need, her body going liquid-soft. The head of his cock probed her anus, pressing forward until the tight muscle released and gave him entrance. She gasped and he entered her, one slow inch at a time. He continued stroking her clit, all the while slowly sinking his cock into her sweet ass. The sensations were mind-blowing, the tightness combined with the fact he could feel every little quiver she made guaranteed that he wouldn't be able to last very long once he was inside her.

"Slow down, baby." He sank in to the hilt, his entire being focused on his cock and the woman beneath him. He leaned forward and nipped the curve of her shoulder. "You may come when you wish."

Continuing the rhythmic caress of her clit, he began to thrust. Her cries increased in volume and intensity as his hips hammered at hers. The gentleness with which he'd entered her was long gone and in its place was pure unadulterated male need. The exquisite slide of his flesh against hers set his senses on fire and all too soon he was lost. He grasped her hips and their cries melded as he came deep inside her.

Several hours later they were sprawled across the bed, the sheets clinging to their sweaty skin. Never in her life had she experienced such an excessive appetite for release. It was as if they couldn't keep their hands off each other and each time was like the very first.

"I think I'm dead," he groaned.

Holly rose, her gaze moving over his handsome features. Was his twin nearly as handsome as Ethan?

"What is your brother like?"

His eyes flew open. "Where did that come from?"

"My mouth," she grinned. "Is he as handsome as you are?"

"We're identical though he wears his hair shorter than I do."

"Is he like you?"

"No, he's boring."

She laughed and sat up. "If he's your twin then I don't see how he could be boring."

He shrugged. "We aren't very much alike. He's a go-getter and I'm more likely to be found behind a computer."

"Oh really." She straddled him. "You seem to be a go-getter to me." Placing her hands across the muscled terrain of his chest, she enjoyed the warmth of his skin against her palms. "You don't have the chest of a computer nerd." She dipped her head to tease a flat male nipple with her tongue.

Air hissed between his teeth. "You think so?"

He reached for her hips and she moved away, shimmying down his body. She ran her hands down his thighs, enjoying the coarse hair tickling her palms. "I do indeed. I dated a few geeks in high school and I don't remember them being as well-built as you are. Especially right here . . ."

She slid her fingers around the thick base of his cock, luxuriating in the silk over steel feel of him. His breath hissed through his teeth and his hips jerked as she ran her thumb along the base of his shaft. She dipped her head and swiped her tongue across the broad tip. He tasted of the sea and warm, virile male. His hips twitched when she stroked her thumb along the sensitive underside of his shaft near the head.

"Holly—" Warning laced that one word.

"I can't hear you . . ." she purred.

A rush of feminine power surged through her body as she ran her tongue over his heated length. He might be her sexual master but that didn't mean she couldn't bring him to his knees. Wrapping her hand around his thick length, she began moving up and down in long, bold strokes as she worked his hardened flesh with her mouth. With each movement, his hips thrust and his breathing grew more strained.

He gave a low, earthy groan and his fingers tangled in her hair. She closed her eyes to concentrate on taking more of him with her mouth. He tried to control her movements, but she resisted his touch, wanting to keep him at her mercy, at her command. His cock jerked against her tongue and she tasted the sweet, salty essence of him. He was close now, very close.

She swirled her tongue around his sensitive head until she elicited an earthy groan from him. Increasing her movements, her hand stroked his thick root as she took him deep into her throat.

"Stop, Holly—" He was begging now.

She ignored him and continued her sensual assault with her

mouth and hand working in unison. Within moments, his body tensed and his hips jerked as he climaxed into her mouth with an anguished groan.

Holly swallowed and continued stroking him for a few moments, allowing him to relax before she released him. She let his cock slip from her lips and she rested her cheek against his thigh before letting her eyes drift closed.

This man had shaken her world and restored her faith in herself. He made her laugh, held her when she cried and all too soon she would have to leave him. She bit her lip and wondered how she would bear it.

Seven

After three days of sensual excess, Ethan knew he wouldn't let her go without a fight. He picked up a thick, silken lock of her hair, the fat curl wrapping around his finger as if to capture his hand in the same way she'd captured his heart.

He'd known even before setting his plan in motion that a great deal was at risk and it had nothing to do with money. The biggest thing at stake was his heart, which he'd lost the moment his lips touched hers. When he'd seen the fear and hesitation reflected in her eyes when he'd broached the idea of them entering into a Master-submissive relationship he'd begun the fall. Only when he'd watched her muster her courage and take his hand was his fall complete.

The major stumbling block to his finally wooing her into his life and accepting his ring was their agreement. On that first night she'd made it very clear that she wasn't interested in having a real relationship. The extent of their involvement would be three days, in bed, nothing more.

The sun was setting outside the windows of their bedroom and while he longed to get out of bed and shut out the outside world, moving just wasn't an option. Holly lay across him like a human blanket, her bright red hair tickled his nose and her soft, sexy snore amused the hell out of him. His fingers tangled in her hair.

Just what did he have to do to gain her love?

Holly concentrated on packing her things. Even though she'd barely worn any of the clothes she'd brought with her, she had taken the time to unpack her toiletries and consequently they were strewn across the marble vanity. Grabbing her hairbrush, she thrust it into her makeup bag to be followed by her moisturizer and deodorant. Her gaze skimmed the gleaming surface of the sink. With her possessions safely packed away, only a damp towel hanging on the rack reminded her that this weekend hadn't been a dream.

She froze when she caught sight of herself in the full-length mirror. Her lips quirked.

No one would know by looking at her that she'd spent her weekend in the arms of a lover. Her long hair was bound into a fat braid and her face was scrubbed free of makeup. Dressed in baggy green sweats, a white T-shirt and tennis shoes, she looked about twenty-five years old rather than a mature businesswoman on the downhill slope toward forty.

She reached for her bag and began pawing through it to locate her lip gloss. All she had to do was grab her clothing then say goodbye to her temporary Master and she'd be home in time to finish up her laundry and prepare for another work week.

Her heart gave a twinge. She needed to speak with him, to see where his thoughts were headed. She'd made him agree that their relationship would be temporary, but would he be open to continuing their relationship? She bit her lip. He certainly seemed to be interested in her though they'd spent very little time just talking. Both had been very aware of their agreement and Holly had been reluctant to get too personal with him. Even though she knew just about everything about him sexually, she knew very little about his personal life.

Just a few days ago she'd thought it was inconceivable for her to ever entertain the thought of a romantic relationship and now, here she was, getting ready to proposition Ethan about carrying on.

She stifled a giggle. She liked him very much. He was intelligent, well-read, and he definitely made her laugh. He wasn't afraid to show his tender side and she knew in her heart that she would always be safe with him. She'd be a fool to walk away without asking him how he felt. Seeing that he'd gone through all this trouble to arrange this elaborate weekend, surely he felt something for her as well.

After coating her lips with the shiny gloss, she rubbed them together then checked her appearance. Her mama always said a lady should never leave the house without her lipstick and perfume—everything else was negotiable.

"Thank you, Mama," she murmured.

Dropping her gloss in the bag, she zipped it shut then headed out to the bedroom. Now to grab her clothing, then—

"Are you almost ready?"

Ethan's voice startled her and she almost dropped her makeup bag. The room was dim and she could barely see him sitting in the corner near the terrace doors. He wore all black and his face was but a pale oval in the darkness.

"Almost." She laid the bag on the bed. "I just need to gather my clothing."

"Can you sit for a moment?" His voice was low, solemn.

"Of course." Her stomach came alive with butterflies and she perched on the edge of the bed. Here it comes. Either he was going to give her the brush-off or declare his undying love for her. She hoped it was the latter.

"I wanted to kill Mains when I heard what had happened to you. Not only had he violated the trust of his submissive, but I knew he'd damaged you in some intrinsic way. It's more than just the scarring of your body, your mind is involved as well." He shook his head. "I've seen it happen too many times with men who think the dominance and submissive lifestyle is a kick, and their lovers can be cast off when they're through. The relationship is about trust and to violate that trust is to violate the very tenets of human nature. For every man who came after, that wall would be a hard one to scale and with each failure, the rows of bricks would increase to the point you'd never be able to see your way out without outside help.

"I'd only seen you that one time, had touched your hand at the costume party, but I was so taken by your smile and laugh. I wasn't kidding when I said I'd become obsessed with you. You'd only said a few words to me and it didn't take any more than that for me. The moment I heard about Mains, your beautiful face invaded every hour of my day and I couldn't get you out of my mind. I spent weeks working on this arrangement, buying the loan, working up the papers." He chuckled. "If my brother ever gets wind of this he'll think I've lost my mind."

"Ethan—"

He held up his hand to stem the flow of words. "Please let me finish. I wanted more than to bed you, Holly. I wanted to help you heal from what that prick did to you. I wanted to remind you that you are an incredible, vivacious, desirable, beautiful woman and Mains never deserved you for a moment."

Tears stung her eyes and she had to place her hand over her mouth to stifle a sob.

"Tell me, Holly, did I accomplish this task?" he asked.

Unable to speak, she nodded as the tears spilled over.

"Good. I'm pleased." His gaze fixed upon hers. "When this weekend began you stated up front that this was a one-shot deal and no future relationship was possible. I'd like to ask you that, after you leave here today, you think about the possibilities of us continuing our relationship." His smile was gentle. "I know I would like to do so as I think I loved you from the moment I first saw you."

Yes!

Holly bit her lip so hard that she was afraid she'd draw blood. On shaky legs, she rose and walked toward him. Stopping by his chair, she sank to the floor at his feet and bowed her head, her gaze fixed on the carpet and a wide smile on her face.

"I'm yours to command, Master."

Epilogue

Monday morning

HOLLY TRAILED HER FINGERTIP over the delicate clutch of violets in a dainty basket-shaped china dish. They'd arrived at her apartment just moments before she'd been due to leave for work and she couldn't bear to leave them behind. A smile danced across her lips. She didn't even have to look at the card to know who'd sent them as only Ethan would've chosen violets.

Her heart swelled at the thought of her handsome Master. He was working late tonight but they'd made arrangements to get together afterward at her place. She planned on cooking a simple pasta dish with tons of carbohydrates to keep them going late into the night—

A screech from below caught Holly's attention.

"You are *not* going to believe this!" Katie's voice rang out through the quiet store. "Come down here, Holly. You have got to see this."

"Oh, my God—" Mel said.

Fearing the worst, Holly ran down the steps. The other

women were standing near the bundled newspapers with a copy of the *Times-Picayune* clutched in their hands.

"What is it? Another politician caught with their pants down around their ankles?" Holly grinned. "Louisiana politics are a mix of a hockey game and wrestling, unconventional and never dull."

"I knew that bastard was as crooked as a dog's hind leg." Katie shoved the paper at her. "You are so better off without him in your life."

"Amen, sister," Mel said.

Holly's breath caught when she saw the front page photograph of Greg "The Bastard" Mains. The headline read, LOCAL BANKER CAUGHT WITH HANDS IN THE TILL.

"It would seem that Greg was arrested yesterday morning by the New Orleans police department on drug and embezzlement charges." Mel shrugged. "Who knew the bastard had it in him?"

"It gets even better. Someone ratted him out and sent evidence directly to the television studio, which in turn notified the police." Katie picked up a stack of books and headed for the aisles. "It just doesn't get any better than that."

Holly almost dropped the paper as Ethan's words came back to her.

"With a little help it can be sooner rather than later."

Could he have done this?

"It would appear that Greg has some very high-placed enemies," Mel said. "Well, to hell with him, and good riddance."

Holly dropped the paper onto the pile to be sold. She felt bad for Doug, but her ex-Master had tried to destroy her business, her life, and he didn't deserve any soft feelings from her. "You've got that right, good riddance."

"Shall I officially open us for business?" Mel picked up the keys and headed toward the doors, her slim hips swaying gracefully beneath her tight leather skirt.

Holly frowned, her gaze taking in her friend's high heels and tight, white shirt. Since when did her friend wear clothing that was so obviously sexy?

"Holly, can you give me a hand in the human sexuality section? That dratted shelf has fallen down again." Katie's voice was muffled.

Holly glanced at the clock. Her workday had just begun but in nine hours and twenty-two minutes she'd be back in Ethan's arms. She headed for the stacks. Now, if she could only find time to run to the local sex shop on her lunch break . . .

His Christmas Cara

SHILOH WALKER

To everybody . . . Merry Christmas, keep the spirit of the season in your heart throughout the year.

My family . . . what do you want for Christmas . . . I'll give you the moon if I can.

One

Eben Marley walked out of the main offices of Venture Advertising, his briefcase held loosely in one hand, his eyes flicking to his watch. The merry calls all around him went unheeded.

Merry Christmas!

Happy New Year!

Somebody brushed a hand down his arm, and a scent he had never forgotten surrounded him.

Slowly, he turned his head, already knowing who he'd see—Cara.

The pretty administrative assistant smiled at him, her eyes not reflecting the smile. A charming dimple winked in her cheek as she brushed her hair back out of her face.

The soft scent of her body drifted to his nostrils and he breathed it in deep, feeling it like a punch in his belly.

Three years . . . He could recall just how long it had been, and his body flared to sudden rampant life.

"Cara," he said, inclining his head at her, lifting a brow as he waited.

Maybe . . . just maybe . . . The thought never had time to complete itself. "I hope you have a Merry Christmas, Mr. Marley," she said before cutting sharply to the right to catch up with some friends.

Mr. Marley.

As she walked away, those words mocked him. A three-year-old memory loomed large in his mind. Just one night—one that had haunted every waking thought for months, until finally, he'd forced her out of his thoughts, suppressing the memory of that night. Except for his dreams.

She still haunted his dreams.

One night . . . that pretty admin, in the elevator at the Grand as he whisked her up to a room where he had fucked her throughout the night, starting with a quickie in the elevator after he'd pushed the stop button. It had ended with him leaving her the next morning with orders for his driver to take her home while he attended to business.

As she walked away, her head bent low against the wind, a memory of that sleek little body wrapped around his, grabbed him by the throat—err, maybe the throat wasn't a good term, he mused as his cock started to throb within the constraints of his underwear and trousers.

Now destined to spend the night hungering for another taste of her, he rolled his eyes and muttered, "Yeah . . . Merry Christmas."

His idea of "merry" was knowing how much money people sank into advertising for Christmas. His company's profits were above last year's, and his own personal bank account was all but groaning.

That was the only thing that interested him about Christmas. Sooner or later, he might slow down enough to have some fun. A rich, husky laugh reached his ears, drifting to him on the wind, as he arrived at the black car waiting at the curb. He stopped, turned his head—the admin assistant, laughing in delight as she accepted a gift from somebody Eben placed as being in accounting.

A night with her definitely would be an improvement over the paperwork he planned to go over. She was grinning with delight as she tore into the present, and he groaned as another image, one he hadn't thought of in years, rushed to the front of his mind . . . that girl . . . Cara . . . sliding him that wide, wicked grin just before she'd closed her lips over his cock.

Tearing his eyes away from her lovely face, he ducked through the car door, telling Jacob, "I want to stop by the bank on the way home."

"Sir, the banks closed at noon today—about thirty minutes ago," Jacob said, his face stiff, eyes blank.

"Closed? Why— Damn it. Never mind, Christmas," he muttered, scrubbing a hand over his face. "Take me on home then. Hell, I should have stayed and gotten more work done."

"Work late? On Christmas Eve?" Jacob said gently. "C'mon, boss. Have a little fun."

Have a little fun . . . Unwillingly, his eyes drifted back to Cara as she threw her arms around the other woman's neck, obviously delighted with whatever gift she had received.

Shaking his head, he tore his mind away from her and laughed, running a hand through his tousled hair. "I make money for fun, Jacob. Let's get moving," he said, sitting back and opening his briefcase, pulling out a handful of files to flip through on the drive.

* * *

Cara Winston glanced over her shoulder as that blond head ducked inside his sleek, sexy Benz and felt her heart flutter. Well, he hadn't growled at her when she wished him a Merry Christmas. There had also been a look of recognition in his eyes, of heat.

Damn it, why in the hell couldn't she stop thinking about him?

Why didn't she hate him?

Hell, now that wasn't really fair. He had told her, right off the bat, *I want sex, one night, that's all.* What gave her the right to still be hurt over his quick and total dismissal the morning after that rather spectacular night together?

No right . . . at all, she reminded herself.

"Give it up, Cara," somebody advised.

Cara glanced back and saw Toni shaking her head. "He's a waste of time," Toni continued. "Hell, this is the first year in the ten I've been here that he finally gave up trying to get people to work on Christmas. And he didn't even want to pay overtime. I can't believe he actually gave us a half day off."

"Well, I had to take it without pay," Chloe said, rolling her eyes. "I didn't have any time left."

Somebody Cara didn't recognize snickered and said, "*Total* waste. I bet the only thing that turns him on is seeing profit and shareholder info, and gross revenue statements."

Cara shivered, her lids drooping. No, that wasn't true. Her nipples tightened as she recalled just exactly how turned on he could get, that raw, hungry look on his face, replacing that cool, blank exterior . . . *No, not true at all.*

Swallowing, she shook her head, shoving those memories away.

She had too much to do, and reminiscing over one wonderful night wasn't going to get it done. Sighing, she turned and hugged her friends. "I've got to go. Duty calls," she said, waggling her fingers at them before turning away and heading for the garage.

Jacob kept sliding him odd glances in the mirror.

At first, as he relived that night with Cara, he hadn't noticed.

But the sensation of being watched sank in, and he looked up with narrowed eyes to see Jacob studying him in the rearview mirror, instead of focusing on the drive as he normally did.

Eben tried pretty damned hard to ignore him. Jacob was the first decent driver he'd had in months, easily. Since he'd fired Tom, he thought. Of course, Tom had kept nagging him about a raise.

Subtly, but hell, he'd given the man a raise six months earlier. He was still driving the same damned distance, still did the same damn thing every day. Why in the hell give him another raise? Especially since he seemed obligated to give everybody at Venture a raise at Christmas.

Jacob had appeared from the agency Eben had contacted about two weeks ago. Silent, for the most part, and respectful, keeping his eyes averted and his questions to himself. Finally, somebody who understood that Eben wanted a driver, not a golf buddy, a drinking buddy, a fishing buddy . . . just a driver.

But those sidelong looks when the black man thought his boss wasn't looking, they were starting to piss Eben off.

He sighed, and flipped through a few more pages before glancing out the window. He scowled as he realized they were speeding down 64 West, toward Louisville, in the opposite direction of home. "So, Jacob . . . Have you forgotten where I live?" he asked casually, mentally tallying up a mark against Jacob. *That's one.* He gave his employees three chances when they fucked up. And three only.

"No, Mr. Marley, I remember where you live," Jacob said softly, flashing him a dazzling grin in the rearview mirror. "It's just . . . time, I suppose . . . that I do what I'm here for."

A cold chill ran through Eben at those obscure words. "You're my driver, that's what you're here for. Now take me home, if you like your job."

Jacob chuckled, a deep, rolling laugh that probably invited others to laugh with him. "This job? Driving you around? No—I don't care for it, in particular. Wouldn't be a bad one, heaven knows it's easy enough. Except you have got to be the coldest man I've ever met in my life. And it's been a long one."

Eben's eyes narrowed and he said, "Jacob, you are pushing it."

The driver laughed. "Boy, *you* are the one who's been pushing it. And you're too damned stupid to even know it, all that money, that brain of yours . . . shoot, you're even a good-looking kid," Jacob mused, shaking his head slightly as he took an exit that led even farther away from Eben's home. They were close to Louisville Metro's city limits now, and home was a good twenty miles away.

"Why, thank you. Now turn this fucking car around, take me home, and I'll cut your check. Your final one," Eben snapped, furious.

Jacob continued on as if Eben hadn't spoken. "Smart, rich, and you're good with people, when you want to be. Yet you're concerned with one thing, and one thing only. Yourself. But that's okay. That's why we're here. To open your eyes. Hold on."

Eben opened his mouth to bellow . . . but Jacob wasn't there. The front seat was empty.

"Mother fuck!" Eben shouted, diving over the seat in a desperate attempt to catch the steering wheel.

The car smashed into something, and Eben went flying through the windshield. How odd . . . it didn't even hurt . . .

Damn it . . . why now? he wondered, and then blackness—

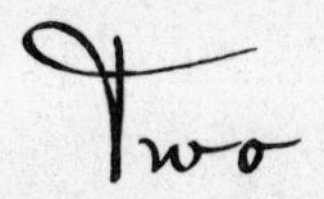

Two

Damn it, she was so sweet, so hot . . . Eben groaned as she levered up away from him, laving his cock with one last gentle stroke of her tongue before she crawled over him, one knee on each side of his hips.

She stared at him as she held his cock steady with one hand, her fingers pale and small against the ruddy flesh of his sex. Eben swore his heart was going to stop in his chest as she slowly lowered herself down over him, taking his dick deep inside the wet, swollen depths of her pussy.

Seating herself fully on him, she planted her hands against his chest, her head falling back. Eben thought his heart was going to explode as she arched her back, the motion thrusting her breasts up, the dark pink nipples tight and beaded.

His cock jerked as she started to move, slowly, lazily, the muscles in her pussy closing around him hot and snug. As she worked herself up and down on his length, Eben cupped the firm flesh of her ass in his hands.

Sleek, sexy . . . she was so damned hot, he thought she'd burn him alive. The air was heavy with the scent of her aroused body, a light sheen of sweat covering her supple curves. He shuddered as she slid up, then down, a fiery trickle of her cream burning his balls as it flowed down.

Damn it, I could fuck her for the rest of my life and never get tired of her, he thought mindlessly.

A soft, silken voice purred into his mind, *Then why did you send her away?*

He jerked awake, viciously, abruptly, his cock throbbing against his belly, pulsating and aching like a bad tooth. His heart was pounding hard and heavy. And he hurt.

Oh, hell . . . he *hurt.* As the dream fell apart around him, Eben grew aware of just how badly he was hurting. And not just his swollen dick, either.

Head pounding, gut churning, body screaming at him in protest, Eben lifted his head, trying to see around him. Too damn dark . . . What in the hell had happened?

He'd been dreaming, that much he knew. Dreaming about Cara. Again.

But what had happened? Where in the hell was he? Not at home, that was for sure. And why the hell couldn't he see anything?

Jacob . . . driving . . . Where in the hell had he been going?

The pain in his head rose up, damn near drowning him, overwhelming the heat from the dream. As the lust-induced fog started to clear, Eben became even more aware of his pounding head. He pressed a hand to his temple, hesitantly, almost afraid he'd find his skull split open. But there were no bumps, no cuts, no wetness that might indicate he was bleeding.

And he could feel his body. Could move—although he sure as hell didn't want to.

What had happened? He didn't remember anything beyond climbing into the car with Jacob—

Jacob had been driving—*shit, where in the hell is he?*

But it was so black, he couldn't see. It wasn't even the black of night. It was the black of a cave, deep in the depths of the earth, the total absence of any light. "Jacob?" he tried to call.

But his voice was barely a whisper. Licking his lips, he started to pat his pockets. There was a light on his cell phone . . . He could use it to find Jacob . . .

Memory rushed back and he froze.

Shit.

Jacob had disappeared. Right in front of Eben's eyes, right after the man had said, *Hold on.*

"Son of a *bitch!*" Eben groaned, fisting his hand and slamming it down . . . and down . . . and down . . . There was nothing under him. No bed, no ground, no rock floor. Nothing.

And as his mind tried to wrap itself around that concept, he started to fall.

A harsh curse escaped him, his body tensing with fear. Arms flailing, he tried to grab onto something, to anything. But there was nothing there.

And still, he continued to fall, his clothes flapping around him, his hair streaming into his eyes, the wind striking his face.

Down and down, until his descent finally seemed to slow, and his clothes stopped flapping. That was the first sign that he might be slowing down—his clothes drifting loosely around him, his hair blowing around his face instead of slapping and stinging his skin and eyes.

A few moments later, his feet landed on the ground. Eben blinked. There was light now, bright blinding light, where moments before, there had been none. It grew brighter and brighter as he stared into it, until, like the sun, it eclipsed, and the light softened.

Now a warm, amber glow cast its light on everything.

Finally able to see, Eben turned and looked around him. He was in a room. Or he thought he was, although there were no doors, no windows. And when he looked up, trying to see where he had fallen from—just a ceiling, a domed, smooth shape that stretched maybe twenty feet over his head.

Bad enough that he'd fallen, now he couldn't see where he'd fallen from. He could have handled that. And he could have figured out how to explain his being in this room, although there was clearly no way out. Like he had been put in a box as the box was being constructed around him.

Yes, he could handle that. Figure it out. Deal with it.

But the soft laughter that was echoing through the room, *that* was a little harder to understand.

Because he knew that laugh.

And the person it belonged to was dead.

"Well, son, you never were one for listening, were you, Eben?"

Slowly, afraid his ears were playing tricks on him, he turned around.

And sitting there, twenty feet away, settled on a couch exactly like that one Eben had found him on the day he'd died, was Eben's father.

Rustily, he said, "Okay, what's going on? Is this some kind of sick joke?"

Taylor Marley laughed again, shaking his head, flashing that familiar old smile. "No, son. Not a joke. It's just me, your dad," he said, smiling at Eben, a smile that seemed bittersweet.

"Not possible. You died. More than fifteen years ago," Eben said flatly, shaking his head. "What in the hell is going on? Who in the hell are you? Did somebody hire you and that bastard, Jacob? You two playing some weird kind of joke?"

"Well, now, that's not a nice thing to say," Taylor said, his mouth twisting into a frown as he stared at Eben. "Jacob isn't a bastard—he's one of the finest men I've met since I came here. And I've met quite a few outstanding individuals."

"Awww, now that's okay," a low, deep voice said, that southern accent as musical as it had been when he was telling Eben to hold on.

Eben whirled, forgetting that his body had been screaming at him moments before, forgetting the pounding in his head.

Forgetting everything but the man who was standing in front of him, staring at him with those dark, dark brown eyes and a friendly smile. Pointing at him, Eben said, "Jacob, you're lucky I don't kick your ass right here. Get me the hell out of here. Now."

"Oh, in good time," Jacob said, smiling.

"In good time," his father echoed.

Eben finally stopped pacing, a growl of frustration ripping from his throat. No damned way out . . . no way *in* that he could see. So how had they gotten in here? Blowing out a soft breath, he decided that didn't matter.

What mattered was getting out.

So he tamped down the anger and the fear he was feeling and went to stand before his father, ignoring the man seated in the armchair next to them, playing solitaire. "What in the hell am I doing here?" he asked without preamble.

Taylor laughed and clapped his hands together. "Damn, it's about time," he said. Then his face sobered and he leaned back, staring at Eben with inscrutable brown eyes. "Did you forget what I told you?"

Don't waste your life . . .

His father's last words to him echoed through Eben's mind, even as he searched his memory, trying to figure out what in the hell his old man was getting at.

"Well, that's an improvement, at least. You admit he is your father and this isn't a joke," Jacob mused, slowly turning over another card and tossing it down before lifting his gaze to meet Eben's.

Eben's eyes flew wide and he whispered, "What?"

"You heard me. And yes, for the record, I can read your mind . . . sometimes." Jacob crossed his arms over his chest, leaning back to stare at Eben with shrewd eyes. "As can your father."

Taylor lifted a brow at Eben and sighed tiredly. "Boy, I tried to tell ya, then. And you didn't listen," he said quietly, leaning his head back.

Eben said forcefully, "I don't know what you are talking about. I'm done with this. Take me home."

"You do know what I'm talking about. I told you not to waste your life," Taylor snapped, standing up and stalking away from them, going to stare at a blank wall. "Don't go trying to search that steel trap of a mind, looking for some other reason. Not when you know damned good and well what I'm talking about. You. Wasting your life."

"I'm not," Eben said, startled by the vague, accusatory glance Taylor Marley shot him. "Damn it, I run a multimillion-dollar advertising business, have a vacation home in California and one in France. I was—"

Taylor waved his hand and spat, "Bah! It means nothing . . . because *you* are empty. When was the last time you were truly happy?"

Eben stilled. He blinked, staring at his father as those words echoed in his mind. Then he shook his head and said, "I *am* happy."

Empty . . . The word resonated through him. *Empty*. He clenched his jaw, and through gritted teeth spat, "I am happy."

"You're not," Jacob said from behind them.

Eben turned and demanded, "How in the hell would you know? You're my driver—or you were. I'm firing your ass."

Okay, Eben . . . buddy, you're sounding crazy. You know this isn't really happening.

Taylor had lifted his eyes skyward and was murmuring silently to himself when Eben looked back at him. A deep, weary sigh escaped the older Marley as he leaned forward, pinning his son with an intense, stark stare. "Boy, this *is* really happening. Deal with it. As to firing Jacob, well, he's already got a pretty good job. I think he'll do okay without yours."

Jacob chuckled, a deep, rolling sound that echoed in the room. "That's the truth. Though I don't know much about earthly ways anymore, I suppose the pay was pretty good. But the atmosphere sucked." He lifted a black brow at him and smiled.

Eben couldn't stop the flush that heated his face. *Sucked, did it?* "Well, that will teach me to let employees have half days off on Christmas Eve."

Jacob laughed, lifting his face to the sky as he murmured, "You are clueless, aren't you?"

Taylor sighed sadly as Eben opened his mouth, closed it, opened it again as he tried to think of what to say to that last comment. "It's my fault, Jacob. I should have raised him a little better, made him understand there's more to life than money, than working. Of course, I didn't really understand that until I met Liz. My sweet angel . . . I miss her."

"Isn't she here with you?" Eben asked. Then he smacked himself in the forehead. "Hell, I'm actually believing this. What is wrong with me?"

Taylor smiled at him. "Relax, son. It's going to be okay—I think," his father said. "Liz is with me—just not here. I've been watching you for the past few months, pretty closely. And she couldn't come. It was tough leaving her, but this is important."

Eben spread his hands and demanded, "What's important? What's going on? What in the hell am I doing here?" Then an awful thought occurred to him and he paled, flinching instinctively as the possibility reared its ugly head. "Am I . . . dead?"

"No, son, but you're running out of time. Either live as you *should* or keep going down the path you're going. And end up alone and lonely," Taylor said.

Jacob said quietly from behind them, "Listen to your daddy, Eben. Clock's ticking. You've got tonight, and then we just walk away. No more chances. And son, without somebody hitting you in the head with a two-by-four, or disappearing in a car right in front of you, you aren't going to try to be different. Not on your own. You've lived like this for more than twenty-five years, and if you haven't changed by now . . . Well, you aren't going to rediscover life at age fifty-five like Marley Sr. did."

Sweat beading on his brow, Eben asked, "What do you mean I have tonight?"

Taylor was silent, cocking a brow at Jacob. The black man crossed his arms in front of him and pursed his lips, lowering his brows, reminding Eben for some odd reason of Sidney Poitier in the movie *Sneakers*. His dark face was serious, solemn, and his eyes just as penetrating as the actor's.

"You have tonight. A chance to look back over your life and see if you're really living it the way you want. After tonight, you'll have a choice, to be *more* than what you are. Or just keep going. If you choose that, that's fine. We won't interfere anymore. But there will come a time, and possibly very soon, when you will regret the choices you've made in life."

Hell, I already do. Hiring you, Eben thought sourly. "So what am I supposed to do tonight?" he asked, jamming his hands into the deep pockets of his coat.

"Just watch . . . and listen. You'll have some guides. Just go where they tell you, and listen to what they have to say," Taylor said, smiling gently.

"And if I don't?" Eben asked, cocking a brow at his father. "If I'm happy as I am?"

"Well, you don't have much choice about whether or not you go with them tonight. You *will* go," Taylor said flatly. "But after that, if you really think this existence of yours can be called happy—so be it."

"You will have three guides—"

Eben interrupted Jacob with a laugh. "Three guides. Oh, hell, this is good. Three guides," he muttered, shaking his head. "You know, with *my* name, I thought I'd heard every joke about the *Christmas Carol* and old Scrooge imaginable. But this is definitely new."

Eben spun around and plowed his fingers through his hair, staring off into the amber light that surrounded them. "Look, Dad, it's not that I don't appreciate your concern, but—"

A deep peal of sound echoed through the room and darkness fell once more, hiding everything from sight.

"Dad!" Eben called out, searching his pockets frantically for his cell phone. Silence . . . no answer. "Dad!"

He finally found the damn phone and tried to remember by touch alone where on the dial pad the button for the mini flashlight was located. But before he could find it, the darkness lifted and he was standing on the street where he grew up.

Only that wasn't possible. They had torn that neighborhood down and put in a golf course. *Years ago.* So how in the hell could he be seeing it now?

His eyes alit on a small boy, wispy blond hair falling into his eyes, the thick lenses covering them magnifying his eyes to damn near twice their normal size.

Holy shit!

"You were such a sweet kid, you know that?"

Eben blinked, his corrected vision graying for a second. Then he turned, his eyes widening as he stared at a statuesque, lushly built woman. Damn, talk about a wet dream . . .

She wore a wine-red robe of velvet, the real kind, his experienced eye decided, with that luster that only silk velvet had. The velvet gleamed richly against the deep cleavage revealed by the plunging neckline. Her skin looked satiny, touchably soft, and Eben felt his fingers itch to touch, for just a minute. Thick black hair waved down past her full hips, and nestled in the dense black waves was a crown made of flowers and . . . *fruit*?

The woman's eyes were a deep, fathomless blue, and they twinkled as she stared down at him. And she *did* have to look down—she must have been nearly seven feet tall.

Eben was about five-ten, so he felt like a damned midget,

much like he had felt through most of high school, until he'd finally shot up from his five-two skinny stature. Well, he had still been skinny, until he'd started swimming and running, finally developing some muscle.

Not that he had a bad view from here—he was on eye level with a very nice, very round set of breasts, and he could smell the seductively sweet scent of her body.

"Ahem."

He tore his eyes away from that lovely set of tits and met her gaze, seeing the laughter lurking there. "I'd be offended, if I wasn't so pleased to actually see a human reaction from you," she said, her deep, throaty voice caressing his ears, stirring his blood. "You so easily ignore women, ignore life . . . ignore everything but the money you love to make. Well, there *was* one woman who made you feel human . . . but we'll get to her later."

As she laughed again, Eben scowled, turning away. That deep chuckle echoed in his ears as he stared at the boy—the long forgotten image of himself as a child. That was back before Mama had left them, running off to be with her rich lover. Eben had learned years later that she had died in a car wreck after she and that bastard had partied it up too much just a few months after she'd left them.

He hadn't known—his dad had figured he'd been through too much trauma already for a five-year-old, losing his mama once. He didn't need to lose her again. "That's me, isn't it?" he asked, his voice oddly husky.

"Yes, it is," she said. Long moments passed as they watched the boy. When she broke the silence again, her voice was soft and gentle as she told him, "I'm your guide."

He snorted. "I figured you were going to say that. Do we really have to live this entire Dickens charade through?"

Again, she laughed, lifting her face to the sun. "It's been a long while since I thought of him," she murmured, a soft smile curving up the corners of that wide, sexy mouth.

"Dickens?"

"No, Ebenezer Scrooge. You share a great deal in common with him—not just your name," she said gently, her eyes softening as she watched the boy stand up, cradling a model aircraft precariously in his hands. "Such a remarkable boy, you were, so smart, so quick. He was, too."

"He *who*?"

"Why, Ebenezer Scrooge, of course," she replied, the expression on her lovely face saying that he *should* already know that.

"That's a fictional character," Eben said, rolling his eyes.

"Hmmm . . . are you so certain?" the guide asked, winking at him. "I remember him rather well. You are so like he was . . . but you are a great deal younger. Too young to be so cynical."

Eben shook his head, at a loss for words. Now he was being told one of the great works of classic literature was based on truth. That was ridiculous. He cocked his head, watching the boy as he carried the model airplane up the sidewalk to the porch of the house. "I wanted to be a pilot," he murmured.

"Yes—I believe you would have been a remarkable one," she mused.

In the blink of an eye, they were at the window of the house, staring in. Eben watched with reluctant fascination as one of the most hurtful memories of his childhood played out before him. Eyes shining, the young child proudly displayed the aircraft to his father, and was rebuffed. His father was too intent on his books, his files, his notes, barely glancing at the model as he scowled. "Ben, I've no time for your toys and foolishness. I have to . . ."

The words faded into the distance as Eben watched the child image of him deflate. "Five-year-olds generally can't do models by themselves," he said thickly. "I tried to get Dad to help me—but he was too busy."

"Hmmm, I know, sweetie," the guide murmured, lifting a long, graceful hand to rest on his shoulder. "You rarely played with toys, did you?"

"There was no point. Toys didn't do anything," he said, his voice husky. Why were his eyes stinging? He wanted, badly, to go up to that boy and hug him close.

"Your father did love you," she said quietly. "He was just hurting so terribly inside."

"Hell, it was just an airplane," he muttered, shaking his head tiredly, blinking away that peculiar stinging in his eyes.

"Was it?" she asked.

The image before them faded away, replaced by an image of an older Eben, one bent low over his books, his young face tightening with a scowl as a merry laugh echoed out. "Eben, all you do is study!"

Bella . . . his throat tightened. Damn it, he hadn't thought of her in years.

As he watched, the younger Ebenezer Marley lifted his head from his books, his thin face drawing tight in a scowl as he stared at his high school girlfriend. Why hadn't he realized how lucky he was to have her? Girls like that never looked twice at scholarly geeks like him.

With her long, thick butter-yellow curls, and sparkling blue eyes, Bella Martin was a high school boy's dream come true—slender, svelte, open. So kind, so sweet, and she had wanted him.

"C'mon, let's go sledding. The snow from last night is perfect—we can go out to Morgan's Hill and sled, then go to Beth's and have some hot chocolate, watch movies," she said, kneeling down by him, running her fingers through his hair, her eyes imploring.

"I don't have time for that foolishness right now, Bella. I've got to get these papers done so I can turn them in after the break. I'll be graduating early, and I've got too much to get done to play," he said dismissively, moving his head away from the distracting caress of her hand.

The boy hadn't seen the look on her face. But the man watching them now saw, and he felt it like a punch in the gut. "That's was kind of shitty of me," he whispered, his heart clenching as her pretty blue eyes filled with tears, not just at his refusal to go and have fun with her, but from the way he moved away from her touch.

She probably wouldn't have understood that it didn't irritate him, it was *distracting*. Her touch, her laugh, the sweet way she smelled made him want to forget everything, and just be with her.

Her lips trembled and she sighed, her voice whisper soft as she said, "Okay, Eben. I guess I can go alone."

"Why in the hell didn't I just go with her?" he muttered, his eyes hard and grim as he stared at the downward angle of his head, the young Eben so focused on his books.

"Much like you are now," she said shrewdly. "Isn't he? Focused on nothing more than studying, while you focus on making money. You don't even spend that much of it. You hoard it. What are you saving it for?"

"Money's too hard to come by to spend it recklessly," he said absently, unaware of how his hand kept rubbing over his chest, right over the ache in his heart.

"Not for you," she countered. "You make money almost as easy as you breathe. When it comes to the business world, everything you touch turns to gold, doesn't it, Ebenezer?"

He shot her a narrow look. "Don't call me that," he said shortly as the world around them faded away, enshrouded in fog.

"Ahhh, you've always hated that name, haven't you? Eben or Ben, doesn't matter which one people call you, as long as it's not Ebenezer." She flashed him a grin, her full ruby-red lips parting to reveal a dazzling white smile. "Not that I blame you. The name *does* sound like it belongs to an old man. Can't understand why your mama named you that."

A cruel joke, he thought sourly, his eyes dropping to the lush mouth of the guide. Then he jerked away, spinning around.

And stared at yet another scene from his past. "No." His voice flat, firm and decisive, he shook his head and repeated, "No. I don't want to see this."

As Bella, older now, her face sadder, stared off into the distance, Eben, now twenty-five and already rich, glared at her. "You're *what*?" he repeated, dismayed.

"I'm getting married," she said quietly. "I met him in France. Remember, you couldn't go with me, too busy." She shrugged, but he could see the echo of pain in her eyes. *Now*.

Then, all he had seen was her turning away from him. "Damn it, how in the hell can you be getting married? *We're* supposed to be getting married."

She gave a watery laugh and asked, "When? First it was after college, then it was after I got a higher paying job at a better school. I've been teaching at Country Day for two years now, Eben. And we haven't even set a date. Now you want to get this buyout done, then we can talk about it. But after that, something else will come up, and I'm tired of coming in behind your desire to make money, baby. I need to come first, for once."

Eben's former self arrogantly said, "You do. Why in the hell do you think I'm working so hard? It's for you, for us."

She smiled sadly. "No, Eben," she said gently, her eyes sparkling with the tears she'd held back for years. "It's for you. I don't need millions of dollars to be happy. All I ever needed was you. Once. Now I need to be away from you. I'll never be happy until I'm free of you—because you'll never be free enough for us to be together, get married, have a family."

Eben's belly tightened with disgust as he watched, knowing what was coming next. "Damn it, can he make you feel like I do?" he demanded, striding over to her, cupping her neck and arching her face up, savaging her mouth as he ran knowledgeable hands over her.

They'd lost their virginities together, and he knew that lithe, toned body like the back of his hand. She whimpered in her throat, her hands fisted at his chest. When she finally tore her mouth away, Eben could see the tears streaming down her face. Both the man he had been, and the man he was now, watched as she turned her face away and whispered, "No, Eben, it's over."

As she walked away from him, the fog closed in, hiding his past self from his view, but the memory of how he looked, shoulders slumped, eyes closed in defeat, lingered. "She would have come back to me, right up until the very last, wouldn't she?" he asked, his voice husky.

The guide sighed, shaking her head as she looked at him. "I don't know, Eben," she said honestly. "Bella loved you, with all her heart. Until your carelessness smashed it, time after time."

The fog lifted and he was now staring in through the window of his penthouse, as he brought woman after woman home with him for a few hours, but never the same woman twice. With every woman he fucked, he sought a replacement for the one he'd lost, and he never found one. Never found anybody that touched something inside him the way Bella had.

Until one night . . . *Damn it.* She would make him watch this.

As he stared at an image of himself lying beneath a sweet-faced girl, he flushed. *Cara* . . .

"Ah, yes," the guide murmured, a smug, pleased little smile curving her lips as she glanced from the scene in front of them to Eben. "There's the girl. Even more than Bella, she made you forget yourself, didn't she? So much so that you pushed her away."

"Stop it," he growled, staring at the image of himself in bed with Cara. His gut clenched, his cock jerked in remembered ecstasy as he watched himself slide his hands up the long line of her torso to cup her breasts. He could remember how she felt under his hands . . . soft, silken . . . perfect.

There had been love in her eyes, naked and shining. That girl had been an assistant in accounting, and had been promoted after just a few months to an admin assistant. For the past few months, she had been working pretty closely with him, and always staring at him with those pretty green eyes. He gave in to temptation one night—taking her to the Grand, wining and dining her—then he had fucked her silly.

The following Monday he'd had her transferred to another department, one where he wasn't likely to see her often, if at all.

Just so he wouldn't have to see that love again.

The final image of her was the one he had shut out of his mind, right as he'd closed the door to the suite on her, after telling her Tom would take her home. She had just sat there, staring at him, her pretty green eyes blank.

The guide whispered, "What is it about love that frightens you so, Eben?"

He went stiff as another scene from his past wavered into view, his eyes narrowing on the image of yet another woman—this one somebody he couldn't even remember. How could he forget a woman who had taken his cock into her mouth? A woman whose thighs he had spread wide while he lapped at her pussy? How is that possible? But he had done it. Slowly, carefully, trying to keep the frustration he felt from surfacing in his voice, he said, "Love doesn't frighten me. It's just . . . useless."

"Useless," the spirit repeated, her voice flat and cool. "Love moves mountains, shatters lives and rebuilds them. Love is the most amazing, and sometimes, the most awful thing known to man. Only love could take a child who was raised by cruel parents and turn him into one of the kindest, giving men. Only love could teach a woman who had known only abuse at the hands of a man, to trust another man, and allow him to teach her true pleasure. Love is many things, but *never* useless."

Eben turned to scowl at her, only to find himself alone. Once more.

Three

When he looked back, he was staring through yet another window . . . and this time at Bella. She'd cut her hair.

That was the first thing he noticed. But then he promptly forgot as he realized what she held.

A baby, a tiny, towheaded baby with thick, golden curls, lashes lying low over smooth cheeks as the babe suckled at Bella's breast.

A deep, warm voice murmured, "See what you gave up?"

Unable to turn and meet this new guide, Eben ignored the spirit as he stared at Bella's face, at the happiness he saw there. His throat locked up as she started to sing quietly, rocking back and forth ever so slightly. She'd always had the most amazing voice . . . Swallowing, he whispered, "This isn't real."

Why did staring at the baby nursing wrench at his heart so painfully?

"Oh, it's real, all right," that voice behind him murmured. "The baby is three months old today. His name is Cameron. And he has a sister who is just barely two."

Two? Whirling, eyes lifted, he opened his mouth to rail at the woman in front of him. Only to still, his hand falling to his side as he stared at the exact opposite of the creature who had just left him. Five feet, *maybe,* reed slender, her mouth painted the color of cherries, her dark chocolate gaze curious, even friendly, as she stared at him. Soft black curls fell into her eyes, over the warm mocha hue of her skin.

She smiled at him sunnily. "Not Morgan, am I?" she teased, that deep throaty voice seeming so at odds with the petite, wraithlike creature in front of him.

"Morgan?" he repeated dumbly.

"Yeah, that tall lady you were just talking to?" she drawled, rolling her eyes at him before sauntering forward. "The Amazon?"

She propped her arms on the windowsill, staring in at Bella. Softly, she said, "She's happy, you know. She rarely even thinks about you, but when she does, she prays. Prays you'll find happiness in your life. But she doesn't even miss you—ain't that sad?"

Absently, he corrected, "Isn't. Isn't that sad?" But he barely even realized he had spoken as he stared in at Bella.

The woman laughed merrily, the rich music of it echoing all around him. "Isn't that sad? I'm trying to teach you an important lesson in life, and you want to correct my grammar," she said, chuckling, her eyes dancing with mirth. "Something is so wrong with that."

Eben scrunched his eyes shut and whispered, "A dream. All a dream and I'll wake up in bed." He frantically hoped, prayed, and wasted his time, because when he popped one eye open, it was to see the second guide—the *spirit*—staring at him with bright, curious eyes. She slapped him on the arm and said, "Calm down, babe. You're gonna wake up, in bed even. Question is . . . how long are you going to wake up *alone*? Wake up lonely, convinced that every ill in life is soothed by the making of money, more and more money? You don't even spend it!"

She smiled, greedily rubbing her hands together. "Damn, if I had some of that money, a real body again, and two hours, that's all I'd need, two hours," she said, wiggling elegantly arched brows at him.

"A-again?" he repeated.

With a whimsical smile, she turned her eyes to him, lifting one small shoulder in a shrug. "I'm dead, Ebenezer. A ghost. What is a ghost, or a spirit, but somebody who died?" She sighed, shaking her head. "But even I lived a better life than you. I was nineteen when I died in that crash. Nineteen. And at least I understood what *happy* was." She shot his long, expensive wool coat a derisive glance. "It wasn't about money, although I did love to spend it."

Sourly, he snapped, "If you are so wise, then show me, damn it. What in the hell is happy? I want this over with."

Those brows rose above her expressive eyes as she cocked her head at him. Without a single word, she lifted a slender arm and gestured, the filmy white gown she wore floating around her limbs and torso as she turned slightly, stepping out of the way.

Eben felt it in his gut like a vicious punch as he stared back through the window. It was still Bella, only now she held a toddler in her arms . . . and in the toddler's lap was the baby. The little girl was smiling with youthful delight as she ran a finger down the baby's button nose, making him grin and coo. Sitting behind Bella, a contented smile on his face, was the man she had left him for.

Bella's eyes sparkled, a smile of peace and contentment on her face, joy and pride all but radiating from her. And when she lifted her eyes to stare at her husband, a look of lust and love entered them, a small smile curving her lips as she dropped one lid in a quick wink.

The warmth of the room, the happiness that filled it . . . the sound of that little girl laughing made his throat tighten.

Okay.

He got the picture. That was happiness. Tightly, he asked, "Can we go? I see your point. I lost her, lost my chance at that. I'm sorry."

The woman laughed, and this time, it was a sound completely devoid of amusement. "Oh, honey, it's not even close to time for you to go yet."

As the fog moved in, Eben lifted his hand and rested it on the glass between him and Bella, his chest tight.

The glass was still under his palm as the fog cleared, but it had changed. The window was smaller, cramped almost, as he stared through it in bemusement. Who in the hell did he know that lived someplace like this? He was staring through the window into an older home, one that was showing its age despite some valiant attempts to maintain it.

A Christmas tree stood beside a window opposite him, tucked in far too closely to a fireplace. The room was tiny, barely big enough for the tree and the old, run-down couch and a dented, scarred coffee table. Eben turned his head to look at the guide, puzzlement in his eyes. "What are we doing here?"

"You don't know who lives here, do you?" she asked wryly, shaking her head. "I'm not surprised, not really. Although the man worked for you for darn near close to ten years. Tell me something, do you even know his wife's name? His middle name? Whether or not he drank coffee?"

"*Who* are you talking about?" he demanded, turning his head back to the window, peering through. Cupping his hands around his eyes to shield out the light that emanated from behind him, Eben pressed his face close to the glass. There was a picture on the mantel . . .

A toddler came running in, tripping over her own feet and tumbling to the ground. Throwing her head back, she opened her mouth and let out a loud wail. A man came into view, chuckling as he knelt to lift the baby, holding her against his chest and rocking her. "Shhhh, Katie, it's okay . . . Got a boo-boo? I can kiss it," he murmured.

Daniel Wilson—what in the hell was *he* doing here?

The man was a former manager of the design department. "I don't get it. What is Dan doing here?"

"Where else would he be on Christmas? He's home, of course, with his family. That's where we all deserve to be on the holidays," the spirit said softly. "Isn't she pretty?"

Eben's eyes were unwittingly drawn to the pretty little girl but he didn't comment about the child. Instead, he said, "I pay my people decent. He was a manager, for crying out loud. He can afford better than this."

"Well, at one time, he *had* better than this. But he gave it up—somebody he loves is very, very sick . . . and the insurance was changed. To a plan that's barely substandard. He's going broke on medical bills and prescriptions," she said levelly. But Eben could see the displeasure in her eyes.

He felt that look, that disappointment, strike him like a fist in his gut. As guilt and shame started to build inside him, Eben licked his lips. "The insurance policy we used to have was too expensive. We have to keep costs down . . ." But why did the words sound so trite as he looked at one of the sharpest minds he had ever worked with?

Because they *were* trite. It wouldn't have affected anything, really, not with the kind of business he did, to keep the better insurance plan. But when Martin Shanning had suggested the cheaper one, well, hell, Eben was all for keeping down costs.

Come to think of it, Dan had made a politely voiced complaint about the change. And Eben had ignored him.

A year later, he'd fired him because Dan had refused some business trips that Eben had thought were necessary. "I can't be gone from my family so long," Dan had argued.

"I'm sorry to hear that, Dan. I wish you luck elsewhere."

Just before Thanksgiving.

The door swung open, revealing a slight, pale child, and woman with weary eyes standing behind her. The glass between them seemed to fade as their words suddenly became painfully clear. "Livvy, honey, you aren't supposed to be out of bed," Dan said gently, shifting the toddler to one hip as he moved to the girl with the overlarge eyes, set in a thin, hollow-cheeked face.

She giggled and said, "Daddy, Santa doesn't want me in bed on Christmas. I'm going to flop on the couch. Mama said I could."

"I thought we were going to bring all the presents up to your room," Dan said, stooping down and lifting the frail child in his arms.

"But it's not as much fun without the tree," she said simply, resting her head on her father's shoulder.

As Dan turned, Eben flinched at the look in his eyes, angry, helpless . . . full of love. He looked so tired.

"What's wrong with her?" Eben asked, almost afraid to.

"She has a congenital heart defect. She's always been too ill to try corrective surgery. Asthma, pneumonia . . . The doctors now think she's finally strong enough to try the surgery. But the insurance is balking about covering it," the spirit said, her voice hard and brittle as ice, her eyes going cold and flat as death. "Daniel is working with several groups to raise money. He wanted to try a fundraiser at work—"

Eben clenched his jaw tightly, self-disgust roiling through him as he recalled Daniel approaching him about possibly trying charitable fundraisers—a lot of employees liked to do them, made them feel good about themselves and their workplace.

And Eben's response? "Then they can go work at a homeless shelter on their days off. That's not what the workplace is for."

"I'm a real bastard," Eben whispered, staring at the family through the window, watching as Daniel passed the toddler off to her mama so he could tuck the sick little girl onto the couch, pulling a blanket up to warm her.

"Yes. Of course, firing him right before the holidays really topped it," the guide said brightly, smiling sunnily. But the look in her eyes as she stared at the girl showed him what she was feeling inside.

Helpless, angry . . . much like Daniel looked.

"I'll hire him back," he whispered to himself. *Change the insurance, give him a raise . . . He shouldn't have to live in this fucking dump.* As the anger churned through him, he asked, "Will it save her? The surgery?"

The spirit shook her head as she sadly said, "Nobody knows. She's got a unique medical problem. The vessels that are supposed to pump the blood to her lungs for oxygen just aren't there. A doctor in Florida thinks he can place vessels there—but it's experimental."

"What about some kind of governmental aid? Won't they cover it?"

"That's where Daniel's gone, finally. His pride wouldn't let him while he was able to do it. But her medical bills are piling up and without a job, he's going to have to declare bankruptcy. And that sort of word will get around. Who wants to hire a guy to help run an ad design department when he can't manage his own finances better than that?"

One had nothing to do with the other, Eben thought, his frustration mounting the longer he stared at the little girl. She was a pretty thing, frail and almost fey; she was so thin. Her eyes sparkled and danced as she tore into her presents with glee, unaware of the looks being passed between mother and father.

"If she *doesn't* get that surgery, this will be her last Christmas," the spirit whispered at his side, rising onto her toes and resting her hand on Eben's shoulder as she spoke. "They know that, as much as they fight against admitting it. But her time is running out. Daniel wanted her to have the world—and he can barely manage to buy presents for his kids at Christmas."

Eben whirled away, pacing, his hands opening and closing in futile rage. *My fault—damn it, this is my fault,* he thought, enraged. Spinning around, chin lifted, he demanded, "Take me back. *Now.* I'll pay for the surgery, I'll pay all the medical bills. I'll give him his job back, with a raise—anything. I can't—"

A knot swelled in his throat, so heavy, so huge, he could barely speak around it.

"I can't—"

The spirit stared at him, her eyes glowing, a tiny smile lurking at her mouth. "Can't what, Ebenezer Marley?" she asked as his voice trailed off.

Turning, he walked back to the window and whispered, "I can't let that little girl die."

She laughed sadly. "Money can't buy everything. All the money in the world won't save her if God decides she's suffered enough." Then she slid him a sidelong glance. "Besides, we're not done yet. There's so much more for you to see."

The fog shrouded them, and then he was staring in through a grand Palladian window, watching the people in the room who were gathered around a white tree, strung with white lights and hung with magnificent golden bows and ornaments. A deep, rollicking laugh echoed through the room, and unconsciously, Eben's own lips curled in response.

The spirit's gaze dropped to his mouth, one raven brow lifting in appraisal.

Eben didn't notice—his eyes were rapt on the man striding past the window, coming to a stop by a small child playing by the tree. "My cousin—Joshua Marley," he murmured. "He asked me to come over for Christmas."

"Yep," the spirit said, a sardonic smile curving her lips. "He sure did. Even though his wife told him not to. She doesn't care for you, Eben."

No. Eben agreed in silence as he watched said wife come into the room, wearing a rich burgundy velvet gown. Tracey couldn't care less for Eben, hadn't been able to think kindly of him since she'd heard he had ordered a thorough investigation of her after Josh had proposed. He'd just been looking out for his cousin—one of his rare sincere acts for somebody other than himself.

But it had been an insult to her, he realized now. *She loved Joshua,* he thought as she walked up to the huge, bearlike man and wrapped her arms around him, smiling up at him.

"You haven't heard from Eben, have you, Tracey?" Joshua asked, stooping down to lift the boy into his arms.

"No, baby," Tracey said, rolling her eyes before she leaned over and kissed Joshua on the cheek. "You need to just give up on that guy, Josh. He doesn't care about anybody but himself and his money."

"Now, Trace," Josh said, sighing, shaking his head.

She held up a hand, eyes closing for just a second. "I'm sorry. You're right—just because he's a cold, calculating bastard doesn't mean we should think uncharitable thoughts toward him," she said flippantly.

"That wasn't exactly what I was thinking," Josh said, chuckling. "But . . . Eben's a lonely guy. I bet he doesn't even realize how lonely he is."

Tracey smiled warmly up at Joshua, wrapping her arms around him. "Hmmm . . . and he thinks he's the rich one," she whispered. "We've got so much more than he'll ever have."

"I'm not giving up on him," Joshua murmured.

Outside, Eben felt his throat tighten, his eyes stinging. *Thanks, Josh.* "He's a good guy," he murmured to the spirit.

Only she wasn't there.

A chill ran through Eben as the glowing light dimmed, and the air around him grew colder and colder.

A whisper of sound ran through the air, a sighing—deep, desolate, and cold. *Indeed* . . . a voice whispered, the word seeming to come from everywhere and nowhere at the same time.

He is the only one who would truly mourn you, if suddenly you were gone.

Eben whirled around, staring into the thick gray fog, trying to find who was speaking. "Where are you?" he demanded, his heart slamming against his ribs.

The wind whistled, blowing at his coat, whipping his hair around his face as he peered into the grayness.

Well . . . perhaps this is *another.*

The voice was low, with an odd, almost hissing sound, slithering against his skin, and the sound of it made melancholy rise within him. As the fog lifted, he saw a woman—with a short, sleek cap of black hair, a spiky fringe of bangs falling into a pair of green eyes that had been laughing the last time he saw them.

The time before that? Blank, empty . . . right before he'd closed the door and summoned his driver to pick her up from the hotel.

It was Cara, her head bent low against the wind, her shoulders slumped, grief etched onto her face. There was just sadness now, no husky laugh that drew people to her, invited them to laugh with her, no wicked smile. Just grief.

Why would she miss him?

You have a talent . . . for making people love you, without even trying. And then you destroy it. Those last words were whispered with a low, mean hiss that sent shivers down his spine.

This newest spirit didn't like him—the others may have been disappointed, but this one had a rampant dislike of him. Eben could feel it.

A cold, cruel laugh echoed around him and just behind him, to the side, right at the edge of his peripheral vision, he saw somebody move. Turning, he found himself staring at a hooded figure. It was a woman. Under that spidery gossamer weave of her gown, he saw a woman's form—firm, small breasts, sleek hips, long thighs—but her face was obscured by the hood. All he could see was the cold blue gleam of her eyes.

"On the contrary," the guide murmured, and her voice was that chilling rasp that made his skin crawl. "I like you, and people like you, quite a lot. People like you always come to me with a scream of disbelief, as though you cannot understand why in the world you landed in my cold, desolate domain."

Eben swallowed, squinting as he tried to discern the face within that enveloping cloak. "Are you the final spirit?" he asked in a low, gritty voice.

"Indeed. Look at the woman you could have had—if you had just offered a simple smile," the guide whispered, holding out a slim, pale hand and pointing.

For a long moment, he couldn't even move—her skin was translucent. He could see the shadow of the bones that made up her hand. Shaken, he lifted his eyes and stared back at Cara's lowered head, his eyes tracking where she stared.

A gravestone.

She was standing at a grave—

Holy shit!

Somebody called her name and Cara lifted her head, letting Eben see the sparkle of tears in her eyes. Somebody came trudging up through the snow covering the ground. The guy was familiar, but Eben couldn't place him.

"What are you doing here, Cara?" the guy asked, staring down at the headstone, his body blocking it from view.

"Doug, go away," she said, her voice weary.

"I want to know, damn it. We've been going out for three months. I don't like this obsession you have with a dead guy."

Cara lifted her eyes, her chin going up. "We stopped dating three weeks ago. I broke it off, remember?" she said coolly. Then she moved her eyes back to the headstone. "And I can't explain my obsession, as you call it. There was just—something about him. He called to me."

Those words faded away as Cara's form slowly faded away.

Eben was left staring at the headstone.

But he didn't need to see it. He already knew it was his name.

Today's date was on it. December 24, 2004.

"If I'm supposed to be dead, why are you showing me this?" he asked, his voice shuddering out of him as a dull, leaden weight settled in his heart.

"That is yet to be seen," she said obscurely. "There's another grave here—somebody you've seen before."

Eben lifted his head with dread. "No."

As he watched Daniel walk across the lonely, empty graveyard, Eben's heart started to bleed—black, bitter blood that he felt spreading through his veins with every beat of his worthless heart.

"Not the girl," he whispered, the hot sting of tears in his eyes. "I don't want to see this!" he bellowed, whirling away. But in every direction he turned, he saw the same tableau playing out before him, Daniel walking alone through the snow-covered cemetery, a gay red poinsettia in his arm, his face lined and weary. He looked twenty years older.

"She died on the table. It took a while for him to raise the money and she caught ill, again. But her heart was failing—they waited months for her to get stronger, and she never did. They decided to take the chance," the spirit said, her voice deepening, and starting to echo. "They lost."

A whisper of a sigh escaped the guide and she said, "The girl is not here though—she went on. The young and the good-hearted usually do."

"Went on?"

The ghost replied, "Of course . . . to there."

Eben followed the direction she was pointing, that long, pale hand with its ghastly imagery of bones visible. His throat swelled as he saw a soft, golden light gleaming in the distance, far away.

"Indeed, very far, for one such as you," she whispered.

Eben's legs went out and he fell to his knees in front of the gravestone that bore his name.

"Tell me you're lying, that the girl didn't die," he said flatly, his heart aching as he looked from that soft golden light back to Daniel.

"She was a weak child, Eben—too weak." Something in her voice made him look up, the echo of grief, the huskiness of tears.

"No," he whispered, thickly, shaking his head.

"No."

four

NO.

No.

No.

The words echoed inside his head. The darkness surrounding him was heavy and oppressive. As Eben finally forced his eyes to open, he found himself lying in his own bed, his eyes on the elaborate metalwork that made up the canopy.

He jerked up, his breath sawing in and out of his lungs in harsh, ragged gasps.

What in the hell?

A dream . . . just a dream . . .

"No, Ebenezer Marley, it's not," said a familiar voice from over by the window.

He jerked his gaze around, eyes widening as he saw Jacob standing there, a pocketknife in one hand, a chunk of wood in the other. "Not a dream," Jacob mused as he started to whittle on the piece of wood, brows drawn low in concentration.

"You." Eben pressed his hands to his eyes, trying to convince himself he really wasn't shaking. No reason to be shaking, it was a dream.

Jacob chuckled. "Your dad warned me you'd be stubborn," he mused, shaking his head. Lifting those sharp, intelligent eyes, he said quietly, "It's Christmas Eve, and you have some choices . . ."

Rolling out of bed, Eben stood naked in the cool air, staring out the window of his grand home—over the lonely estate—as snow started to fall.

Why hadn't he ever realized how lonely it was?

Jacob's chuckle was just a memory in the air as Eben strode to his closet, jerking open the doors and grabbing the first things that came to hand, blue jeans and a heavy sweater, lying folded on a shelf.

And on top of them, he found a small piece of wood, carved into the shape of a child, kneeling by a bed, hands folded in prayer. Carved in tiny letters into the footboard was a word . . . *Choices* . . .

Choices . . . closing his eyes, he remembered that split second of fear that he had squashed as he went flying through the window.

Why now?

As he stared at the small carving, the answer to that question came to him.

Because he had been walking into a very dim, very lackluster future, a cold, empty one. And he'd never even realized it. He had to wonder, even if he had realized it, would it have mattered?

As a thousand thoughts raced through his head, another question passed through his mind. *Why not sooner?*

Because up until just now . . . he didn't think it would have mattered.

Folding his hand around the wood, he held onto it as he jerked his jeans on. Then he tucked it safely into his pocket before yanking the sweater over his head.

Moments later, he was on the phone with his personal assistant, an older, soft-spoken woman by the name of Clarise. She said quietly, "I certainly hope you're feeling better. It's so unlike you to be ill—and so close to the holidays . . . That's terrible."

"Ill?" he repeated.

"Hmmm. I was rather surprised when you called me so late last night, but if you hadn't, I would have worried when you didn't come to work. You needn't worry, sir. Everything here is fine—"

What in the hell? he muttered silently, shaking his head. "Listen, I need some information about a former employee, Daniel Wilson. His address, for starters. And then every known debt that he has. And come tomorrow—no, tomorrow is Christmas—come Monday, I want every single debt paid off. Use my personal company account and say *nothing* to him about it."

There was silence on the other end of the phone. Then, a polite clearing of the throat. "Sir? You want me to pay off his debts?"

"Yes. All of them. And get me the name of the top pediatric cardiologist in the country. No. In the world. I want the best. And soon. Call me on my cell phone—I have some Christmas shopping to do."

On the other end of the line, he was unaware of the shock on Clarise's face as she repeated faintly, "Christmas shopping?"

He had already hung up the phone, striding out of his bedroom as he made sure he had his cell phone. "Jacob!"

Bea, his butler, slid out of a room. A puzzled look in her eyes, she said, "Sir? Is there something you need?"

"Yes. Where is Jacob?"

She frowned, cocking her head at him. Finally, she asked, "Ahhh . . . Jacob? Sir, I don't know any Jacob."

"My driver," Eben said with a frown, staring at her in puzzlement. "I hired him a few weeks ago."

Bea shifted from one foot to the other, looking as distressed as he had ever seen her. "Sir, you've been driving yourself for the past month. Ever since you let Tom go." And although her expression never changed and her voice remained level, Eben could feel the cool displeasure that action had earned him.

"Driving myself?" he repeated. *Hell, maybe I'm losing my mind.* But before the thought had even completed itself, the small piece of wood in his pocket seemed to throb and heat.

Blowing out a sigh, he closed his eyes, running his fingers through his tumbled blond hair. "Okay. Find Tom. I want him back starting Monday, if he is willing, with a ten percent pay increase."

"Tuh . . . ten percent?" she repeated faintly.

"Yes," he called over his shoulder as he jogged down the stairs. "Don't worry. You're getting fifteen."

He heard an odd muffled thud, but didn't look back. If he had, he would have seen his ever graceful butler sitting flat on her butt in the middle of the landing.

"Choices," he muttered to himself as he slid behind the wheel of his car. His hands flexed on the steering wheel and a wicked, boyish grin lit his face. Damn, he'd dreamed about having one of these, just getting out on the highway and opening it up. But he'd never done it—

"What a waste," he muttered, jamming the CLK into drive and speeding down the driveway. Damn, if it was summer, he could open the windows, feel the sun, the wind. Had that ever mattered?

No. Driving fast ate up gas, which ate up money. And why in the hell did that really matter? "Got more than I'll ever spend," he said quietly, his pale blue eyes soft as he admitted that to himself.

What fun was the money—if he didn't put it to good use?

He couldn't remember the last time he'd been to the mall. And he knew he hadn't ever come on Christmas Eve. He knew where it was, out on Shelbyville Road, but he didn't think he'd gone into a mall in more than five years.

"This place is a madhouse," he whispered to himself as he sat staring at the mall from the driver's seat.

Shaking his head, he grinned, a white flash of straight, even teeth in his face as he climbed out, slamming the door behind him. "Might as well dive right in," he said. Then he laughed. "I sound like a lunatic talking to myself."

As his long, lean legs ate up the distance, he plotted out his attack. He always worked better with a plan. The toy store was the most important, but he had to make sure there was a fine spread on the table for tomorrow. Maybe a new briefcase for Daniel, with a big fat check inside . . . and a letter begging him to come back. The check could be incentive, a signing bonus, of sorts, for coming back.

Daniel might accept that.

* * *

On the way out of the mall, with the assistance of a wide-eyed teenage girl helping to carry the bags, he saw a store set up in a trailer just outside. The rich smell of smoking meat carried to him on the wind as he recognized the name of the small catering place.

Perfect . . .

It took several hundred dollars, but he convinced the manager of the store that he really needed that ham tomorrow. With a soft sigh, and a look heavenward, she offered, "I can have one ready tonight—it will take a while, but . . ."

"That would be wonderful," Eben said, grinning widely at her as he tucked the money into her hand. It was after he had driven away that she realized it was five hundred, not the three hundred he had initially bribed her with.

Now, he just needed somebody to play delivery boy. The stuff had to get to Daniel's house tonight, but Eben was a little leery about showing his face just yet. Tomorrow, he'd face Daniel.

Not tonight.

five

CARA STRETCHED HER ARMS high overhead, looking out over the sea of bent heads, her heart wrenching as she heard a young giggle. In the corner, Mac McGowan was playing Santa to a small group of youngsters. The oldest was probably five. Much older than that, growing up the way these kids did, and the kids didn't want to go to a stranger. Even some of the young ones were leery of the man in red, but Mac won them over.

He'd been doing it for years, even with her. Sighing, she pressed a hand to her back, stiff and aching from spending so long on her feet. *Why do you keep coming here, Cara?* she asked herself.

This same shelter, every Christmas, for more than five years.

Sixteen years ago—she'd been twelve—was the last year she had spent having to eat at one of these tables. The year her mother died, leaving her with nobody and nothing in the world. Not that she'd ever had much even with her mom. They'd lived on the streets more often than not, after her mom had taken Cara in the middle of the night, running away from an abusive husband.

They'd eaten in shelters, lived in the old run-down car . . .

stolen food. Then her mom had died and Cara was alone, and she'd never tried to beg for food. Her mom had warned her, a kid alone would get taken by the state. So she stole, and she crept into the shelter with larger groups of people, hiding among their numbers. And for a while, she'd gotten by.

Mac was the one who had finally called Social Services, and she had been taken, kicking and screaming, to foster care.

It had saved her life, made her life. And it had only taken ten years for her to find her way back here to look Mac in the eye and tell him *thank you.* He had smiled, that sweet smile she remembered, only now in an older, wearier face.

Her parents, the people who had taken her in and later adopted her, had been dead for three years, from a car wreck driving home from vacation. But before that, they'd spent two Christmas Eves here with her, serving up the simple, hot food to the people who wandered in through the doors.

Her dad had collected money at his workplace and bought presents for the kids. Simple toys, dolls and cars, things easily tucked into a pocket. And Cara and her mother had led clothing drives to collect enough decent coats.

She really needed to be able to walk away from this, though. It was breaking her heart, looking at the small children, the mothers with weary, hopeless eyes, so lost and broken. And Cara could do nothing.

Her lashes dropped and she sighed.

Nothing, because there wasn't enough money to do what needed to be done.

Money. The root of all evil, so it was said, and that had to be true. How else could something so trivial stand in the way of helping people? Wasn't that the most important thing?

People, and not numbers stamped on paper.

Money . . .

As Eben slowed to a stop, he tried to figure out exactly why he was stopping. Why he had taken that exit, one that had led him clear into Louisville's west side. Geez, he never came down here. He wouldn't be able to tell north from south down here.

So why in the hell was he standing in front of an old church? Why did he feel like this was where he needed to be?

"You're losing your mind, Eben," he muttered, running a hand through his hair as he climbed out of the car, frowning as he glanced around. *I'm nuts, leaving my car in a place like this . . . It's not even going to be here when I get back.*

He stepped through the door, assaulted by the smell of unwashed bodies, filth . . . and despair. Eben didn't realize such a human emotion could be recognized just by breathing in the air.

As he looked around, he saw tired women, some of them with battered faces, all of them with a weary, resigned look in their eyes. Older people, gray-haired grannies who should be at home in rocking chairs, men sitting on the floor, dog tags around their necks, their eyes dark, haunted.

And kids. Damn . . . the kids . . . so many of them.

And it was from the kids that he realized there was more than just despair in the air.

There was also life, and hope. Laughter coming from some of those kids as they crowded around a Santa who laughed and chuckled as he watched the sparkling, dancing eyes of the children. There was the smell of hot, simple, nourishing food, and . . . *pine.*

Pine trees . . . With a small grin, he studied the massive tree in one corner of the large rec room, his eyes roaming over the twinkling lights and the decorations, many handmade, most likely by the kids at Santa's feet. Boughs of pine draped from the exposed rafters, intertwined with sparkling white lights.

Damn, it had been years since he had seen a *real* Christmas tree, one obviously decorated by those meant to enjoy it. And he'd forgotten how much pleasure just looking at a Christmas tree could give him. That had been . . . years ago, not since he had been a teenager.

A low, husky laugh drifted to him through the cacophony of sound. How he heard it, much less recognized it, made no sense. But as his head whipped around, he knew who he'd see.

He also knew, with a bone-deep certainty, exactly why he was here.

It was for her.

That smile of hers—seductively sweet and wicked all at the same time—had haunted him for months, until he'd forced himself to simply stop thinking of her. It had taken all of his willpower to do it, all of his focus to think of something, somebody other than her.

She had intruded upon his mind at the oddest of times, so he had done what he had thought was best and forced her out of his thoughts.

What *would* have been best would have been to seek her out, beg her forgiveness for the way he had treated her . . . and try to forge some sort of relationship with her.

And that was why he had been drawn here tonight.

Choices . . .

Drawing the small carving from his pocket, he rubbed it with his thumb. He had made the wrong one so often now that it seemed that was all he knew how to do. Maybe that was why it was so hard to take a slow step in her direction . . . and then another, followed by another . . .

Cara felt the intense gaze on her neck as she held out the plate to the bent old man in front of her. He had fought in the Vietnam War, she knew, from past conversations with him. His fiancée had left him while he was gone, clinging to the peace movement of the sixties.

He had come back, hurting inside, but looking for the girl he had loved all of his life, thinking everything would be okay . . . but it hadn't been.

After that, somewhere along the way, he had simply given up—and now he was here, smiling that sweet smile at her before he made his way over to a table and dug into the food with hands that shook.

Scanning the tables, she searched for the source of those watchful eyes, but saw only people eating their food, kids with proud smiles showing their small prizes to their grim-eyed mamas. She frowned and shrugged, turning her head to check on Mr. McGowan. He was getting older—it was in the tired way he moved, the occasional tightening of his face as his body pained him.

But right now, he was having the time of his life. With a smile, she looked back to the line, reaching for the ladle . . . and then she froze.

Slowly, Cara turned her gaze back to the entryway of the church's rec hall.

Eben . . . she mouthed, her heart tightening in her chest.

He was staring at her with intent, watchful eyes. As she met his stare, a rare, solemn smile edged up the corners of his mouth. She swallowed and turned her eyes back to the lady in line, staring at her in bemusement.

Behind her, Cally Anders chuckled. "He been staring at you like that since he walked through the door five minutes ago, girl," the older woman drawled, grinning as she reached around and took the soup ladle from Cara. "Go on, already."

"He's not here to see me," she said faintly. Even though she had dreamed for months that he'd come after her . . . somehow, in the few short months she'd worked with him on a takeover project, she had fallen in love with him, and that one wild night together had only intensified her feelings.

However, Eben didn't return them—that was evident in how easily he'd walked away, how he'd transferred her out of his department, how he'd ignored her for three years.

But Cara took off her apron and tossed it on a table, walking out from behind the counter, her eyes held by his. Something about that intense stare had her heart pounding, her mouth going dry. Curling her hands into loose fists, she jammed them into the pockets of the brightly colored Christmas cardigan she had pulled on with her jeans.

Coming to a stop before him, Cara forced her lips into a casual smile. "What brings you to Bethel, Mr. Marley? You lost?"

A different light entered his eyes. "I was. I'm not now, but thank you," he said quietly in that polite, cultured voice.

She pondered that for a moment, her mouth pursed as she studied him. "Okay . . . I give up, Mr. Marley," she said, shaking her head. "What are you doing here?"

Her breath locked in her chest as he took a minuscule step forward, lowering his head to whisper softly, "I realize I didn't conduct myself in the best manner, but don't you think you know me well enough to call me Eben? You did then."

Blood stained her cheeks bright red as he lifted his head and met her gaze. "Ahhh . . . That night was an anomaly—didn't change anything, remember?"

"Oh, I remember that night," he said obliquely. "All too well." He looked away, studying the people around him with unreadable eyes. "What brings you here?"

Touching her tongue to her lower lip, she wondered what he'd say if he knew her real reasons. She hedged, shrugging casually as she said, "My parents and I helped out here for a few years. They died three years ago, but I keep coming."

"I'm sorry," he said, sliding his pale blue gaze back to her, an odd light in it. He looked almost—sympathetic. But she hadn't thought sympathy was an emotion Eben Marley could feel.

Her throat tightened. With a silent nod, she acknowledged his words. Long moments passed before she forced herself to speak. "You never did say why you were here . . . Eben."

His gaze swung back to her; his lids drooped low over those indescribable blue eyes. It fell to her lips for a long moment before he met her stare again. "Would you believe me if I said I didn't know what I was doing here?"

Not a lie, really. Until he had seen her dark head bent over the counter, he *hadn't* known what he was doing here.

She nibbled on her lower lip with small, white teeth, her eyes narrowing as she scrutinized him. He had half expected a slap in the face from her, but she didn't seem upset to see him . . . he could even feel how *un*-upset she was. See it in the way her lashes dropped to shield those pretty green eyes from him. In the way her breathing had picked up as he lowered his mouth to murmur in her ear.

The scent of her flooded his head, and he was half drunk on it.

Spreading his hands wide, he said, "I've never been here in my life, never even heard of it—I was driving through Louisville and just had this . . . urge, I guess you'd call it."

Dubiously, she said, "You don't strike me as the kind to follow a whim very often."

He wasn't. She had been one of his rare ones, a sudden, driving need to feel her beneath him, to feel just how hot and tight her pussy would be as he went down on her. Most of the women he slept with were ones he had seduced, with the only goal from the get-go being to ease the driving need to fuck.

She had been different, though, watching him with those wide eyes, trying to hide her attraction for him, never once approaching him . . . until that night. He didn't like being approached; he wanted to scope out what he wanted, move in and take, plain and simple. Any time a woman tried it the other way, she got shot down.

Not Cara though.

Lifting one shoulder in a shrug, he said thoughtfully, "I've been thinking that I need to listen to those little urges more often." Then he focused his gaze back on the patrons of the shelter. "Can I help?"

The laugh that bubbled out of her throat had him lifting a brow at her. She muffled the giggle, falling into silence as she looked at him. "You want to help . . . *here*."

A frown tugged at his lips as he studied the people there, his heart tugging as he looked at one shy little girl who kept staring at Santa with yearning eyes. But every time her mama urged her to go, she would bury her face, clinging for dear life. "I don't necessarily think *want* is the correct term. But I *need* to," he said finally.

A dull sense of shame rushed through him as she cocked her head at him. "Are you feeling okay, Eben? You're not acting like yourself."

He laughed, a dry, humorless sound. "I don't think I've ever felt better, if you want the truth. And I've never acted less like myself in my life."

So she showed him the ropes, all the while sliding him odd little glances that she thought he didn't see. He ended up in her place, behind the counter, serving people hot, homemade soup that smelled better than anything had in quite a while.

Well, besides Cara.

The simple potato soup smelled like ambrosia, and Eben tried to recall the last time he'd had something as simple as homemade potato soup. Too long, he decided a few hours later as he dug into the bowl somebody had urged into his hands.

Cara was out mingling with people, talking to the women and the older folks, cuddling babies, a smile on her lovely face. And although she tried desperately to hide it, he saw the echoes of grief in her eyes.

She didn't want to be here.

He waited until the last person had been served, the last present given from Santa, before he approached her. The people were slowly drifting out, one by one, and Cara was bent over a table, gathering up bowls and plates, a forlorn look in her eyes.

"If being here bothers you so much, how come you're here?"

he asked, straddling a bench as she walked by, reaching out and laying a hand on her arm.

Cara stilled, her eyes dark in her pale face. For a long moment, she was silent, staring into the distance, seeing nothing.

Finally, she lifted her gaze to him, shrugging halfheartedly. "Would you believe I have to be here?" she asked, echoing his question from earlier. "Not everybody has a warm home, a loving family. I have to do what I can to make it a little better for them."

He cocked a brow at her, his heart tugging as the lost look he had glimpsed on her face throughout the night resurfaced. "It seems to me to be a little more than that," he said quietly.

Cara's eyes narrowed and he felt the chill emanating from her so strongly that he wished he'd kept his mouth shut. "Hmm . . . you think you know me well enough to make that sort of statement, Eben?" she asked, her voice brittle.

He blanked his face, rising slowly. With a single nod, he said, "You've got a point. I never took the chance to get to know you, did I?" He forced a smile for her and said quietly, "Have a Merry Christmas, Cara."

He felt her eyes on him the entire way to the door, where he retrieved his coat from the coat rack. Without looking back, he walked out the door.

And what a pleasant surprise—his car was still there. And it even appeared to be in one piece.

Cara could have kicked herself. "Damn it, how stupid are you going to get, Cara?" she muttered to herself, heading to the door seconds after it swung closed behind him.

He was just ducking low to climb into his car as she shoved

the door open. As he caught sight of her, that straight blond brow lifting as he met her gaze, Cara felt her heart tremble.

There was something in his eyes she hadn't ever seen there before.

Humanity, she supposed. An empathy and understanding she suspected was very foreign to him.

She also suspected that her last remark had cut him. Cara couldn't help but feel a *little* pleased over that. After all, he had snubbed her pretty badly a few years ago. Crossing her sweater-covered arms over her chest, she walked up to him, studying his face.

He closed the door, propping his elbows on the roof of the car as he looked at her. "It's cold outside, Cara. Go back inside."

"Why are you here, Eben?"

A slow smile spread across his face as he shrugged. "You wouldn't believe me if I told you," he said, lifting his face to the dark, winter sky.

"Try me," she offered, shivering in her sweater as the wind whipped down the cold streets. *What was going on here?* she wondered.

He came from around the car, shrugging out of his coat. She closed her eyes in bliss as he wrapped her in it, the warmth seeping into her bones, his scent covering her. Her nipples peaked and stiffened as he ran the back of his knuckles down her cheek.

His eyes . . . Damn, she could get lost in his eyes. They had always been mesmerizing, that pale, ice-blue gaze. But today had been the first time she had ever seen warmth in them.

Not sexual heat, that was different . . . but *warmth*. Something so simple, so human . . . and very unlike him.

His other hand came up and he cupped her face, staring

down at her intently as he lowered his head, stopping when his mouth was just a whisper away from hers. *"You . . ."* he murmured just before he slanted his mouth across hers.

The taste of him exploded through her, a gasp falling from her as she arched up against him. He stroked his tongue teasingly over hers as his hands slid down from her face to wrap around her waist, drawing her against him. Her nipples burned inside the silk of her bra, throbbing and aching. One long-fingered hand slid down to cup her ass, bringing her firmly against him.

Cream drenched her panties, and just like that, she was ready for him. He could have urged her into the backseat of his car and she would have gone willingly. Against the soft curve of her belly, she felt his sex throb—the feel of him against her made her pussy ache.

She started to whimper and moan, deep and low in her throat, as he pumped his hips against her belly. A growl rumbled out of him as he pulled his mouth away from hers. His free hand slid up and fisted in her short cap of hair, pulling her head back and to the side, exposing her neck to the sharp, hungry press of his teeth.

"Your taste—I've never forgotten," he rasped.

Shivering, she lifted her lashes as he sighed roughly, pulling away from her just a fraction. Unwittingly, her tongue slid out, capturing *his* taste on her lips. Her lashes fluttered closed as she savored it.

Forcing a breath into her lungs, she opened her eyes, watching him as she lifted her hand and pressed her index finger against his lip. "I never forgot yours," she replied in a husky whisper.

The pounding of her heart seemed to roar in her ears as he opened his mouth and bit down lightly on the tip of her finger, stroking it lightly with his tongue.

But his next move simply left her floundering. He released his grip on her finger and drew her up against him, one hand cupping the back of her neck, the other arm wrapped firmly around her waist, holding her snug against him. Slowly, she wrapped her arms around his torso, stroking the long, powerful lines of his back with one hand, wondering yet again . . . *What is going on?*

"I had you reassigned because I didn't like how often you kept creeping into my thoughts," he whispered gruffly. "Nobody has ever lingered in my mind for more than a day—until you."

He moved away then, pacing over to the curb, his shoulders stiff with tension as he stared into the night.

"Eben—"

He whirled around, his eyes hot on her face. "You stayed with me, even after that, do you know that? Your face would slide into my dreams at night, when I didn't have any control. I fantasized—very briefly—about convincing you into some sort of . . . arrangement, if you would . . . Anything so I could see your eyes go black as you started to come," he murmured.

Her eyes flashed with indignation as he moved in on her, his hand coming up to cup her chin. "I wanted you, but I wouldn't have whored for you," she said coolly, her eyes narrowing to slits.

"Hmmm . . . Maybe that's why I never asked," he said, quirking a brow at her. "Or maybe it's because I was worried I'd do quite a bit to convince you to come to me. Your face haunts me . . ."

Her heart rolled over in her chest as he repeated himself, shaking his head as though he didn't understand it.

He lowered his lips to brush gently against hers and then he was gone. "Go back inside, Cara," he said gruffly, striding over to his car and jerking the door open again.

His eyes lingered on her face until she did just that.

Six

His hands were shaking as he drove away.

Eben gripped the steering wheel as though it were the only thing anchoring him. Damn it, she was still as sweet now as she had been then. He'd held her in his arms, kissed that sulky mouth, spread her thighs and lifted her ass in his hands, plunged his tongue deep inside the well of her slick, snug pussy, and watched the glory of a climax break over her.

Then he'd walked away from her, pushed her away—of all the foolish things he had done, Eben was certain that this had to be one of the worst. How could he have given that up? How had he thought he didn't *need* just that in his life?

"Well, boy, before now, you didn't realize just how necessary that was."

"Damn it!" Eben bellowed as his father wavered into view in the seat beside him. His foot slammed down on the brake as he cut his eyes to the right and stared at the image of his dead father.

In a hollow, echoing voice, Taylor said with a grin, "Ebenezer Marley, I swear, you look like you've seen a ghost!"

"Damn it, Dad, are you trying to give me a heart attack?" he demanded.

Taylor chuckled. "No need to worry about that—not now. You finally figured out what you needed to know, and I think you're going to be fine," the older Marley said, smiling fondly at his son. "I'm sorry, son. This is my fault, in part. I never raised you to believe there was anything other than the job and the money. By the time I understood that myself, you were already walking down your own road."

Eben scowled to hide the swell of emotion inside him. "I made my own choices, Dad. For a very long time. You aren't to blame."

Taylor sighed, lifting one shoulder in a shrug. "That's the job of a parent, Eben. Listen, don't forget what you've learned today . . . and go get that girl."

His words were still echoing in the car, but Taylor Marley was gone.

And Eben had a gut-deep feeling that it was for good this time. He wouldn't be seeing his father again . . . on this side of life.

With a tight throat and stinging eyes, Eben let off the brake and started back down the silent street.

It was a long drive from West Louisville to the posh area outside of town where Eben lived. Cara hadn't exactly figured out what she was doing. What if he threw her out? What if he laughed at her?

What if he wasn't home?

Or what if he was . . . and he was with another woman?

A soft voice inside her heart whispered that wasn't going to happen. Eben had stared at her in a way no man had ever looked at her before—like she was the center of his universe.

When she finally reached his house, it was late, very late, nearly midnight. She lifted her eyes to the dark sky, staring at the stars that hung like diamonds in the air. Her breath escaped her in a puffy cloud as she tried once more to quell the nerves in her belly.

This was so not like her.

But he had been acting so—not like Eben.

He seemed more approachable, more alive. And his hands, his mouth . . . He had clung to her like she was the only thing in his world. Even that one night together years earlier, there had been a part of him that was disconnected, unmoved by everything—and he had loved her in an almost clinical, focused manner, as though he was determined to make her scream X amount of times, as though he was measuring each response.

Earlier, when he had kissed her, she had been the only thing in his world.

Something told her that was very, very unusual for him. And it was that quiet little urging voice that she was listening to right now. She planned to blame that little voice if she got tossed out on her butt.

The long, paved road wove around Eben's estate. It had been four years since she'd been here, at a business dinner meeting, working with her new boss, meeting Eben for the first time.

And it was as amazing now as it was then, the windows, and there seemed to be a thousand of them, all sparkling under the light of the full moon. The moon hung low and fat in the air, casting its silvery light all over the sumptuous estate. There were more lights blazing, even though it was later now than it had been then.

So he was awake, she figured, nibbling nervously on her

lower lip as she slowly walked up the ornate walkway. *Egads . . . even the sidewalks are fancy,* she thought as she glanced down. She'd been too much in awe of the house to notice anything else when she had come here that one and only time.

Pressing a finger to the doorbell, she took a deep breath, trying to compose herself. Hell, maybe the butler would turn her away—she never doubted there'd be a butler there. Even if it was past eleven o'clock on Christmas Eve.

So when Eben himself opened the door, bare-chested, his pale blond hair tousled, she was at a loss for words.

Except for . . . *Damn, he's hot . . .*

Unconsciously, her tongue slid out to wet her lips as her eyes drifted down the hard, sculpted wall of his chest.

Finally, she tore her eyes away from those six-pack abs and lifted her gaze to find him watching her with an arched brow, a bemused, questioning smile on his face. Her eyes rested briefly on that mouth, one corner canted up, the hint of a dimple in his cheek.

"Merry Christmas," she said finally, keeping her hands fisted in the pockets of the long, rich velvet cloak she'd pulled on. One of her few indulgences, the sumptuous thing was made of real silk velvet, with that soft sheen only the best of velvets had. It lay against her naked body, the wind snaking in under the hem to nip at her bare legs.

He grinned a little wider as he said, "You've said that once already, today, haven't you?"

She shrugged and the edges of the cloak shifted just enough—she watched as his eyes cut to the front of the cloak for the quickest of seconds, hot and intent. When he looked back into her eyes, it was with a bland gaze. But she'd seen the flames.

"Maybe, but I didn't give you a present," she said huskily.

He frowned, brows dropping low over his eyes. "You don't need to give—"

Interrupting, she asked, "Don't you want to know what it is?" And with a naughty little smile, she reached up and flipped open the heavy pewter clasp, shrugging her shoulders so that the velvet fell away. She caught the heavy length in her hand and just stood there, waiting, as he stared at her scantily covered body with hot, hungry eyes. The red push-up bra gleamed against the pale ivory of her skin, the temporary tattoo she'd applied the day before rested right above the line of the skirted garter belt she wore.

Skinny little garters held up the opaque black stockings, and she wore the high-heeled, red fuck-me shoes she had bought on a whim a few weeks earlier.

His voice shook slightly as he rasped, "I don't think I've been good enough for that kind of present." Then he grimaced. "Unless you just plan on letting me look before you walk away."

The cold rippled down her skin and she shivered, but kept her arms hanging loose at her sides. With a slight smile, she said, "I wasn't planning on doing that."

Her breath left her in a rush as he grabbed her and jerked her against him, whirling around as he kicked the door shut. Before she could so much as gasp for a breath of air, he had his mouth slanted demandingly across hers, his tongue driving deep inside as his hands palmed her ass.

Moaning in delight, she wrapped her arms around his neck and tangled her tongue with his. Her nipples stabbed into the silk of her bra, hot and tight and burning. Pussy wet and aching, she rocked her hips against his pelvis, sobbing into his mouth as he lifted her and started to grind his covered cock against the thin silk of her thong.

"Damn it, you're so fucking wet and hot, I can feel you through my jeans," he groaned against her lips. He turned her around, leaning her back against the door as he pulled away.

Her body trembled, crying out at the loss of his heat, but she almost whimpered as he sank to his knees in front of her. "I shouldn't be doing this," he whispered. "I treated you like hell . . . I don't deserve to so much as even look at you."

Cara opened her lips to . . . do something, anything to keep him from pulling away, but before she could, he leaned forward and pressed his mouth against the silk that separated her pussy from his tongue. Agile fingers flipped open the garters and her breath caught again as he slid his hot hands under the short, formfitting, skirted garter belt. The heated, calloused flesh of his palms cupped her butt, lifting the silky, deep red fabric and baring the skinny swatch of silk that ran between her thighs.

He nuzzled her through the thong before he pulled it aside, leaving her sex bare. She heard him groan like a man offered a feast after a famine and then his hands were on her thighs, spreading them, reaching behind her knee to lift one leg and drape it over his shoulder.

His tongue, silken and fiery hot, stabbed at her clit, working it with teeth and tongue as he started to push two fingers deep inside her. She felt that hungry growl that rose from him in a vibrating caress of breath that left her dazed with an embarrassed sort of pleasure.

She could make this arrogant, cool man into a hungry, ravenous being of need and desire . . . *Her.*

A soft, hoarse keen fell from her lips as he shifted position and started to fuck his tongue in and out of her weeping cleft. Her belly tensed, and her nipples tightened painfully as he worked her closer to that bright, shimmering edge of climax.

Wet, hungry noises filled the air as he drank her cream down and lapped and suckled at her flesh. A fist of sensation shot through her time after time with each silken lash of his tongue, until she was rocking her hips against his face, her hands fisting in his hair, riding the waves of pleasure as she started to come.

Cara felt her legs buckling beneath her and she didn't care, barely even realized that he supported her weight as she fell, screaming out his name, her voice rough and hoarse.

As the shudders continued to course through her body, she started to float down to earth, the world actually moving around her . . . and then she realized that *she* was moving, not the world, as he guided her down, the silk of her cloak between the hard floor and her back.

Her lids fluttered closed and she just hummed under her breath with pleasure. His hands ran up the length of her thighs, beneath the snug-fitting garter belt, hooked over the waistband of her thong and slid it down.

And she just . . . floated.

His hands shaking, Eben tore open the fly of his jeans before he levered his body over hers. "Open your eyes," he demanded gruffly, staring down at her flushed face, a sated, smug smile curving her lips. As the heavy fringe of her lashes lifted, he wedged his hips between the soft, satiny skin of her thighs, brushing against her entrance with the head of his cock.

The satiny heat tempted him and he groaned, pushing more heavily against her, shuddering at the contact as the head of his cock breached the dew-slickened lips of her pussy, sliding just barely inside.

Damn it, he hadn't fucked a woman without a rubber in years, not since . . . Her name escaped him, a woman he'd been certain he'd never forget, but as he stared into Cara's flushed face, at her desire-clouded green eyes, he couldn't think of anything beyond her.

"Rubber," he gritted out, trying to remind himself.

Under him, she hummed, sliding her hands down over his ribs, cupping them around his hips and whispering, "No . . . just you . . . just me . . ."

Swearing shakily, he tried to remind himself of all the reasons that wasn't a good idea . . . but couldn't think of a single one, not when she lifted her hips, forcing an aching inch of his cock inside. Not when she dug her nails into the taut skin of his ass and pulled him against her. With a hoarse whisper, he sank home, feeling the satiny wet heat of her pussy close tight and snug around him.

Rolling onto his back, he gripped her waist, rocking her back and forth, his breath left him in harsh ragged pants. She sat upright, driving her weight further down on him, her eyes fluttering wide, a startled little gasp escaping her. Then a smug little feline smile curved her lips and she started to ride, sliding her hands up her torso, over her breasts, before she laced her fingers behind her head, her lashes drifting down.

Eben had never seen a sight so lovely, so erotic, in his life. His heart squeezed in his chest, then seemed to expand as he arched his hips up, pushing harder and harder into her silken sheath, his cock pounding, throbbing—harder than he had ever been in his life. A soft sob escaped her and she braced her hands on his chest, leaning forward and lifting her weight. He growled softly as she pulled up, and he gripped her hips, certain she was going to pull away, but all she did was drop her weight back down on him, taking his cock inside in one fast, deep stroke. Then she lifted, dropped back down, taking him inside her pussy again, and again . . . faster and faster.

Staring up at her, his eyes locked on her face, he watched as she ran her tongue over her lips, a soft purr falling from her mouth. He stared at her hands as she slid them over her torso, up to cup her breasts, then on up until she could run her fingers through her hair, her eyes slitted and glittering in the dim light of the foyer.

The muscles in her belly worked as she rocked against him. As he moved his gaze downward, he could see the slick, wet flesh of his cock as it disappeared back inside her snug sheath. He watched for a long moment as she rode him, so sweetly, so fucking seductively that he thought he'd climax with every damned stroke.

Gritting his teeth, Eben fought not to come, to stay just *there* as she continued that slow, steady rhythm. His balls drew tight, his fingers dug into her hips, his teeth clenched, a spasm of agonized pleasure jolting through him. Fucking her, especially like this, skin to skin, was like trying to fuck a lightning bolt, and he didn't know if he could survive a pleasure this hot, this intense and all-consuming. The cream-slicked tissues of her pussy were fiery hot, tight, flexing around his cock with each breath she took.

"Damn, you're going to kill me, Cara," he gasped out as she lifted again, slower this time, teasingly.

Dimly, part of him saw the shocked pleasure roll over her face, but he didn't comprehend it as he started to arch into her teasing strokes, his fingers biting into her flesh as he forced her back into a hard, fast rhythm. She gasped out his name, and her pussy clenched around him with a viselike grip, the creamy, wet heat of that embrace so tight, so snug. With a savage growl, he rolled, taking her under him, and plunged into her depths as his head swooped down and he took her mouth roughly. Her back arched, driving her tightly beaded nipples into his chest—hot, aching little points of sensation everywhere her skin touched him.

Feeding at her mouth, he fucked his cock in and out of her hot, wet little hole, growling in animalistic pleasure as jolt after jolt of sensation raced down his spine until he couldn't take anymore. The climax grabbed him by the throat, by the balls . . . by his heart as she sobbed his name. The bite of her fingers into his skin, the feel of her coming around him triggered his own climax. Eben erupted inside her just as she tore her lips away from his and screamed out, *"Eben!"* as she climaxed around him with almost vicious intensity.

On and on, his seed jetted into her depths, the milking sensations of her swollen pussy drawing it on forever. With a shaking sigh, as she finally spent him, he lowered himself onto her body, sliding down until his head was pillowed between the smooth globes of her heaving breasts.

"Best present I've ever gotten," he whispered, sliding one hand up until he could link it with hers.

Seven

Cara felt her heart contract almost painfully as he lifted his head and stared down at her through misty, almost dazed eyes. "Stay with me?" he asked, and he lifted her hand to his lips, pressing a kiss to it and watching her over their joined hands.

Stay . . . He wanted her to stay . . . Now *that* was the best present she'd ever gotten.

Because something told her Eben didn't invite women into his house, especially not for this, and never to stay, even for just a night.

She lifted up onto her elbow and pressed her lips to his mouth, whispering softly, "Yes, I think I'd love to."

A startled giggle left her as moments later he stood and swept her into his arms, Rhett Butler–style, carrying her up the staircase, his eyes intent on her face. A dreamy smile curved her lips, as the strength of that act touched something female deep inside of her.

After all, how many women have dreamt of being swept up and carried away, just like this?

Cara definitely had, and so many of her fantasies had been centered on Eben, since the first time she had met him. But she'd never expected it to happen, although she knew exactly how powerful a body he hid under those power suits of his.

Resting her head on his shoulder, she closed her eyes and reveled in the moment, barely blinking as he laid her down on a plush, heavenly bed, the mattress molding to her body like a hug.

"Open your eyes again, let me see you," he whispered gruffly, the mattress shifting just slightly as he lowered himself down beside her.

She lifted her lashes and stared at him, bemused, as he stared back at her as though she was the focus of his entire life. He lowered his head, brushing his lips down the slope of her breast, his breath caressing her flesh, tightening her nipples once more into aching buds. "I really think I'd like to keep you," he murmured, his tongue darting out to wrap briefly around her nipple.

His eyes gleamed like blue fire in the dim light of the room as he lifted his head to stare down at her. "Usually if there's something I want, I just offer up enough money—but I don't think that will work with you. I don't *want* that to work with you," he whispered, and there was that odd, bemused look on his face, in his eyes, as he gazed into her eyes. "But what will work? I totally failed the last time there was a woman who mattered to me, and I don't think she made me feel what you do. I couldn't make her happy, couldn't keep her . . . So what do I do to ensure that I'll make *you* happy? That you'll want to stay?"

Her lips curved into a tremulous smile, and tears stung her eyes as she cupped his face in her hands. "Maybe you should just try asking . . . *later,*" she whispered, her voice husky and rough with emotion. "I want to savor every last second of this . . . and I want you to be sure."

His lashes drooped, hooding his eyes. A slight smile curved his lips and he murmured, "Well, at least that's a chance."

For her, there was little choice. Her heart was already his, she knew. She just wasn't so sure she wanted him knowing that until she was more certain of him—thus, the need to take it slowly. Rising, she pressed her lips to his, pushing lightly on his shoulders until he rolled onto his back.

As he rolled, she held still, breaking the contact with his lips, her eyes running over the firm, lean muscles of his body. A guy who seemed to spend all of his time in power suits really shouldn't look that good. Lightly, she traced the pads of her fingers over his pecs, sweeping down to stroke his hard belly before she moved lower, cupping her hand around the fullness of his erection. Feeling the hard, steely length jerk in her hand, she lowered her head and pressed a soft kiss to the tip.

Watching him from under the veil of her lashes, she took the crown of his cock into her mouth, rubbing it with her tongue as she moved her head in a slow, steady rhythm, licking away the come and cream that had dried on his cock. Humming under her breath in appreciation, she took him farther inside her mouth, until her lips were spread tight around his width and the head of his cock was bumping against the back of her throat.

His hands buried in the short strands of her hair as he started to rise against her, his eyes intent on her face, his jaw locked, a tic pulsing in his cheek. Pulling away, she flashed him a cheeky grin and asked, "Like what you see?"

"Hell, yes," he growled, using his grip on her hair to tug her back down.

As she took him back inside, she felt him shudder, and she couldn't help the internal smile that spread through her, that rush of feminine pride. With her hand wrapped around the base of his cock, she sucked on him, pulling away to teasingly lap at the clear drops of fluid that seeped from him. Lowering her head between his thighs she caught a patch of sensitive skin in her mouth, drawing on his sac and listening as he blistered the walls with a rough curse.

Cara grinned at him mischievously as she lowered her head, taking his cock inside her mouth, deeper and deeper, until the rounded head of his sex butted against the back of her throat.

In a blur of motion, he spilled her onto her back, staring down at her with a stark look of hunger on that poetically handsome face. With his knee, he pushed her thighs apart, driving inside her with one hard, deep thrust, his teeth bared, head thrown back so that the cords in his neck stood out.

With harsh, short digs of his hips, he sank inside her, quick, almost brutal thrusts that sent her shooting straight to the top as a sudden harsh orgasm ripped through her. Sobbing out his name, she locked her legs around his hips, pumping her pelvis in time with his deep, powerful thrusts, the muscles in her pussy gripping at his cock.

He slanted his mouth across hers, stealing her breath away as he plunged his tongue deep inside her mouth. One hand came up, plumping her breast, pinching and rolling the nipple between his fingers. Each pluck from his fingers arrowed down through her belly, tightening inside her womb.

Then hot, brilliant lights exploded in front of her eyes as his hand left her breast, stroking down her side to cup her ass, his fingers straying to caress the tight pucker of her ass. She screamed into his mouth as he pushed against the tight rosette, a forbidden, naughty pleasure she had dreamed about for years. Like a geyser, she came, cream pouring from deep inside her to coat his cock, his balls, and her thighs.

Eben gritted his teeth against the silken spasms in her pussy, the caresses driving him insane, until he couldn't take any more and flooded her hot little pussy. As she said his name again, this time in a soft, dazed whisper, he collapsed atop her and rolled to the side.

Slowly, they drifted to sleep, wrapped around each other.

Cara woke and stared at the elaborate canopy over her head, trying to figure out where she was. It wasn't a sensation she was unused to, not after so many years of living on the streets and then bouncing through foster home after foster home. But it had been years since she had woken up in some place other than her own bed—three years to be precise.

That one night with Eben . . .

Eben! Her eyes widened and she sat up, her gaze flying across the room.

As she encountered Eben's thoughtful blue gaze, she flushed, her heart starting to slam against her ribs.

"Hi," she whispered, uncertain of what to expect.

A soft smile canted up one corner of his mouth and he said, just as quietly, "Hi. Sleep well?"

Nodding, she tucked the sheet around her breasts. "Wonderfully, thanks."

Eben rose from the chair he had been lounging in and climbed on the bed, crawling across the lake-size width of it until he could kneel by her side. Her eyes locked on his face, nerves battling with the lust that was brewing in her belly. Her breath caught as he reached up and laced the fingers of one hand through her short cap of hair, angling her face up.

"I . . . I uh, I haven't brushed my teeth," she muttered, turning her head aside.

He laughed and caught her chin with his other hand as he lowered his head and slanted his mouth across hers. "I don't care," he rasped, rubbing his lips against hers, teasing, then deepening the kiss, plunging his tongue hungrily inside her mouth. Cara whimpered, reaching up to curl her hand around his wrist.

He pulled away, his eyes hot and hungry on her face, trailing one hand from her chin, stroking his finger down the long line of her neck.

And her belly rumbled.

Her eyes widened and blood rushed to her cheeks, an embarrassed laugh escaping her. He chuckled, sitting back on his heels, his eyes glinting as he said, "I guess you're hungry."

Sinking her teeth into her lip, she shifted and nodded. "I can wait a while though. I can eat when I get home," she murmured.

A golden brow cocked and he shrugged. "You could do that, I guess . . . although I was kind of hoping you'd eat here. Unless you have plans for Christmas Day."

"Christmas! Geez, I forgot," she said, laughing and running a hand through her hair. A sad smile curved her lips and she shrugged. "My parents died a few years ago—I didn't have any other family, so it's just me. I was invited to dinner tonight at a friend's, but . . ."

"I've got some things I need to do today," he said, his eyes moving past her to stare at the wall thoughtfully. "Important, and

I have to do it alone . . . but I'd love it if you stayed for a while. Breakfast, at least."

Grinning, she said, "I'd love to."

Of course, she hadn't been expecting him to *cook*. But he did, and he did a damned good job, she decided as she dug into a Mexican-style omelet with gusto. "A man who can cook—a woman's dream," she teased.

Eben smiled, shrugging absently as he sat down across from her. "My mom died when I was young. It was just Dad and me. And he didn't cook very well." Grimacing, he added, "Until I was about ten or eleven, I didn't realize you could do much with that shiny metal box in the kitchen—you know, the one that gets hot."

She grinned at him. "You've got a sense of humor, Eben. I never realized that."

He laughed at her, reaching to flick the long silver and black bead earrings that dangled from her ears. "I did a good job of hiding it," he replied. He took a bite of the eggs piled on his plate and shrugged. "Been a while since I've done much cooking, but not bad."

"Delicious," she corrected him, taking a heaping bite.

"You ought to try my steaks," he murmured, pushing the food around on his plate absently. A sigh escaped him and he set the fork down, leaning back in the chair, just watching her.

Under that intent scrutiny, she squirmed in her chair. "Aren't you hungry?"

A sensual smile curved his lips and he said in a low, husky voice, "Not for food."

Her cheeks heated and she licked her lips nervously before taking another bite. "Can I ask you something?" Keeping her eyes on her plate, she waited until he responded with a "yes" before she took a deep breath and blurted out the question that had been on the tip of her tongue ever since yesterday at the shelter.

"What's going on with you? You act so—different. Sort of the same, but at the same time, not the same at all." Then she sneaked a quick look at him, her nose wrinkling as she asked, "Does that make any sense?"

The look on his face, one of regret so strong it damn near brought tears to her eyes, made her wish she hadn't asked. After a long moment when she didn't think he was going to answer, he finally ran a hand through his hair and said quietly, "I had an . . . epiphany, of sorts. And I feel like I've been walking in the dark for most of my life, and somebody suddenly turned on the lights."

A thoughtful frown crossed her face. "Living in the dark how?"

Instead of explaining that, he said, "You know, a few months ago I fired my best man in the design department. He had taken more time off than I allow employees. He always had his work done, but still. And then I told him he needed to go out of town on some business trips that would take him away from home for a month at a time. He wouldn't go, so I fired him. You know Dan Wilson?" She heard him swallow, saw his eyes close as he folded his hands around his coffee mug. "He has a sick little girl . . . You know that?"

Cara whispered quietly, "Yes. Livvy. I've heard about her."

"What kind of bastard fires a guy, one with a family, just because he doesn't like the idea of going out of town for a month at a time?" he asked softly, his pale blue eyes bleak and cold. "He worked for me for *ten* years—I never knew a damned thing about him except that he had a sharp mind and he didn't cost me money."

Cara's heart wrenched at the emptiness she saw in his eyes.

He slid her a quick glance, his lips twisting in a self-deprecating smile. "Real class act you spent the night with, huh, Cara? Of course, you ought to know what kind of class act I am. After all, look at how I treated you."

It still stung, thinking of that night. But she was coming to understand that he had been scared, and had shoved her away because of that fear. That didn't make it right, but it did make it understandable. A little less painful. Silent, she reached for the exquisitely cut crystal glass of orange juice, drinking a little to wet her dry throat. To do something with her hands. As she tried to formulate something to say to him, he laughed, the sound dark and humorless.

"You can't think of anything to say to me, can you?"

Her eyes softened and she whispered, "Oh, Eben. You know, everybody does some things in life that they aren't proud of. They're not unforgivable—*if* you don't keep repeating them."

He snorted derisively. "You have no idea just how many things I've done that I'm not proud of, Cara. My list of sins is immeasurable."

Cara laughed. "Your worst sins, Eben, stem from being a little too selfish, a little too greedy . . . and just living with blinders on. There *are* much worse sins—killing, stealing from the people who provide for you, adultery, beating and abusing those you should have taken care of." Her throat went tight as long-suppressed memories tried to slip into her mind. "Nothing you've done is something that you can't move past."

"How can you be so sure? You don't even know the half of it," he muttered, pressing the pads of his fingers to his eyes.

He looks so weary, she thought. Sighing, she replied, "Because you *want* to move past it. If you want it enough, you will. The people in life who truly matter will see a different person, if that's what you want to be. A person can forgive a great deal, when it matters." Rising from her chair, she walked around the table, bending down and wrapping her arms around his neck and shoulders from behind. "You matter."

His hand came up, folding over hers. "You're amazing, Cara. You know that?"

She laughed. "Thank you—twenty-eight years of practice."

Craning his head around, he looked at her. "I thought you were twenty-six," he said, frowning. "You were twenty-four . . ."

His voice trailed away and a dull flush stained his cheeks. Cara giggled, leaning down and pressing a kiss to his cheek. "Yes . . . and I turned twenty-five a few months later, and that was three years ago. Today's my birthday, if you can believe that."

He arched a brow. "Happy birthday," he said softly. He shifted until he could reach around behind him and draw her into his lap. Cuddling against the warm wall of his chest, Cara listened to the steady sound of his heartbeat, smiling as he started to rub her back. "Don't you have something special to be doing for your birthday? A party? Family to visit?"

A sad smile curved her lips once more. "I don't put much into birthdays—I love the holiday season, the rush and wonder of it. But since my parents died . . . and my friends want to spend their day with their families. If they knew I was winging it alone, several of them would pitch a fit. But I'm used to it."

"You shouldn't be," he murmured.

Her heart flipped as he cupped her chin in his hand, lowering his mouth to kiss her gently. "Maybe I could take you to dinner tomorrow," he said softly, his voice hesitant.

"I'd like that," she said. Lowering her head back to his shoulder, she sighed as his arms folded around her. "So what exactly are you doing today? Can't be business, not on Christmas." Gently, she teased, "Not even you tried to make us work on Christmas Day."

He laughed dryly. "No. Just Christmas Eve, the day after Thanksgiving, the Fourth of July," he said sourly, but his eyes glinted at her. "It's sort of business—going to see Dan. See if he'll take his old job back . . ." A hint of a grin lit his tired face and he added, "I'm going to do something I've never done before. Play Santa Claus."

She laughed, squeezing his neck. "Sounds like fun. I love giving presents . . ."

Eight

Cara smiled at him, waggling her fingers before she shifted the car into reverse. Something inside him felt hollow . . . damn it, he didn't want her leaving.

But she didn't need to see him eat crow, now did she?

Going to be hard enough to do it without an audience, he thought grimly, shaking his head as he turned and headed back inside the house. All he did was grab a coat and his keys, knowing that if he stayed too long he'd talk himself out of it.

Once on the road back into Louisville, Eben glanced at the map, making sure he was heading in the right direction. He had been assured that the presents had been delivered, along with the food, by Michael, a bright-eyed, idealistic kid who worked as a runner at Venture. Michael was one of the few people who weren't swayed by Eben's grim demeanor, always laughing and inviting everybody to laugh with him.

It was just after eleven now, hopefully too early for lunch, but late enough that they had their morning to themselves.

As he slowed to a stop in front of the ramshackle old house, he blew out a breath. No time like the present.

* * *

It was so easy, he thought later, as he let Daniel talk him into a cup of coffee. Following him into a small, cramped office, Eben sat down on the single armchair that had been crammed into the room, along with the desk and chair in the corner.

So easy . . . Daniel had taken one long, slow look at him after he'd opened the door to Eben's knock. Just one look . . . and he had known where the presents had come from, where the food had come from. A slow smile had lit his face and he just shook his head before standing aside and letting Eben come slowly into the house.

"I learned long ago not to question a gift horse," Daniel said from the chair at the desk. "But I can't pretend I'm not curious as to what is going on, Mr. Marley."

Eben's eyes dropped to the briefcase at his feet, a smile lurking at his mouth. *Well, I had a visit from some ghosts, and they took me through* A Christmas Carol *and I've learned the error of my ways* . . . He laughed silently at the looks he'd receive if he told people that. They'd have him committed, no doubt. So he just stuck with the same line he'd given Cara. "I had a revelation, that's all." He snagged the handle of the Italian leather briefcase, pushing it at Dan. "Here. This is for you. Before you open it, I want you to know that I would like you to come back to Venture. With a raise. And I'm getting the old insurance plan back. But regardless of your decision, the gift is yours to keep. And I don't want to hear anything else about it."

Daniel frowned thoughtfully as he ran his hands over the briefcase. "I enjoyed my job there. I hated being asked to leave. But I can't travel—"

"You won't have to. Travel for my employees is now strictly

optional, with the exception of myself, the VPs, and a few other key people," Eben interrupted, shaking his head. "I'll be offering incentive pay to those who want to travel, but those who can't won't be penalized."

Daniel's brow arched. "Mr. Marley—"

"Eben," he corrected.

"Eben . . . I don't really understand what all this is about, but I'll be damned if I'm stupid enough to pass it up," Daniel said as he popped the latch on the briefcase.

The look on his face was almost comical, Eben thought, as Daniel reached inside with a shaky hand to pick up the check. "It's not certified. Usually I wouldn't give a check of that amount unless it was certified, but I couldn't get to the bank in time yesterday. But just let me know when you want to go to the bank and I'll go with you . . ." Eben's voice trailed off as Daniel lifted his eyes to his face.

"I can't take this," Daniel said, his voice rough.

"You can. You have to," Eben said flatly, leaning back in the chair and hooking an ankle over his knee. "You've lost that much money, easy, in the past year since I switched the health plans."

Daniel's eyes narrowed. "I haven't spent fifty grand over the past year," he said sharply.

"No? How come you sold your old house? Your Benz? And you're still in debt. Take the money. Pay off the doctor bills. *Use it,*" Eben urged. "I know about Livvy's medicines, her health condition. I know she has to have surgery. *Use the money.*"

The look in Daniel's eyes would live with Eben for the rest of his life . . . like some massive, painful weight had been lifted from him, setting him free.

* * *

She is the prettiest, funniest little girl, Eben thought later, as he let them talk him into staying for lunch. With those dark, large eyes dominating her face, and a sharp sense of humor that was already a match for her father's dry wit.

As Livvy ate slowly, she talked with Eben, about school, about Christmas. About herself.

"I'm sick," she said bluntly as her mother urged her to drink a little more, eat a little more. "Did you know that?"

Under her intent gaze, Eben shifted, feeling like he was being called in front of the principal or something. How could a child have eyes that wise? That mature? Softly, he said, "Yes. I know that."

"I have to have a surgery soon, or I'll die," she said baldly, wrinkling her nose up as she pushed the peas around on her plate.

Eben's eyes flew to her mother's face as the woman made a soft sound. "Mama," Livvy said softly, reaching out and wrapping her small fingers around her mother's hand. "I know about it. And I'm not too scared. But I'm going to be okay. I'll get the surgery and things will be fine. But I can't pretend like I don't know."

"It's always good to be prepared for things," Eben said, his voice tight and rusty. "But I bet it hurts your mama a lot to think about it."

Livvy glanced at her mama and sighed. "I know. I just . . . I don't like it when people act like I'm normal and healthy. So I want everybody to know."

Eben's heart went out to her, at the desolate look on her face, the wistfulness in her voice as she said, "I want to be normal . . . and healthy. I want to go back to my old school and I want to see my friends. But I can't. I have to be homeschooled, because I kept catching everybody's colds and stuff. And I can't go to the mall, can't go see movies . . . and all my medicines and my doctor visits cost so much money. Mama and Daddy think I don't hear them talking about it, but I know."

"Livvy," her father said gently, arching a brow at her.

"Well, I'm not going to act like I don't know why we sold the old house," the girl said, acting a little more like a child as she poked her lip out and sat back in the chair with her arms folded. "We just couldn't afford it there anymore. I know that's why you sold your car, and why you drive that old clunker."

Before Daniel could say anything, Eben leaned forward, propping his elbows on the table and staring at her. "Your mama and daddy don't care about those things, Livvy. They care about you. And what's going on isn't your fault—sometimes there isn't anybody to put the blame on. You were born sick. Nobody made that happen, any more than they made you have the prettiest gray eyes I've ever seen, or gave your sister those pretty curls. That's just how it is. But that doesn't mean you're stuck with being sick . . . or stuck here."

By the end of the afternoon, Eben was convinced he was in love with the two little girls. When he went to leave, his eyes stung as both of them demanded a hug. A hug . . . had he ever hugged a child before?

Livvy felt so frail as he wrapped one arm around her shoulders, and the baby smelled so sweet, so innocent. Looking into her dimpled face, he felt something inside shift.

Clearing his throat, he handed Katie back to her mama before he walked outside into the cold, biting air. After Daniel promised to be at the office on Monday, Eben climbed into his car.

There was someplace else he needed to go . . . but he had to do something first.

Cara.

He had to go get Cara.

He was going to his cousin's house, finally, for the first time since his father had died. He was going to a family Christmas—and he wanted Cara there with him.

Cara wandered through the house, feeling bluer than she usually did on Christmas. For a while, there had been happy, family Christmases for her . . . but since her parents died, she had been going it alone.

She was so damned tired of being alone.

For a moment, she pouted. She would really have liked to spend some more time with Eben today. Cara could have gone with him—but if he had wanted her with him today, he would have come.

And that thought just made her even more depressed. At first it seemed like something was happening there . . . her heart insisted something *was* happening. But if a guy had feelings about you, wouldn't he want to be with you on Christmas?

Yeah, she knew Eben didn't have a normal view of holidays . . . but still . . .

As a knock sounded at the door, her breath caught and her heart started to slam and dance inside her chest.

Maybe.

* * *

As Eben pulled into the small apartment complex where she lived, he wondered at how his heart started to slam at the thought of seeing her, how his gut tightened, his head spun . . . how his cock hardened. She'd done this to him almost from the get-go, and he had buried it, tried to ignore it, or shoved it away, whatever seemed to work the best. He had even tried to fuck her out of his system, that one night.

Fat chance. He could touch that sweet body for a thousand years and he'd still want more. Crave more. But after just one night, he'd tried to walk away. Tried to ignore that nagging, insistent voice in his heart every time he had looked at her.

No more. He wasn't ignoring how he felt anymore. He wasn't going to focus on what his head was always whispering . . . he'd start listening to the rest of him.

Hell, if he had listened to his heart three years ago, he never would have pushed her away.

But three years ago, he wasn't sure he would have had a chance at keeping her. What happened yesterday, during the night, the visits from the ghosts had changed him. And maybe, just maybe, those changes would be enough to make her want to stay with him.

When she opened the door a few minutes later, the delight in her eyes struck him like a fist in the chest, knocking the breath from him. Forcing a smile, he said huskily, "I thought maybe you'd join me for dinner at a friend's."

As she reached out and threw her arms around his neck, Eben sighed, burying his face against her neck and just breathing in the scent of her. Her lips brushed his cheek and, blindly, he turned his face to hers, catching her mouth with his and tangling his tongue with hers.

In full view of everybody, he reached down and gripped her hips, boosting her up until she locked her legs around his waist for balance. Never taking his mouth from hers, he stumbled into the apartment and shoved the door closed with his foot as he turned and braced her back against the wall, pulling his mouth from hers and trailing a hot line of kisses down her neck.

Her hands raced up his shoulders to dip into his hair, holding the short strands eagerly as she pressed against his head. He heard her whimper, low and soft, as he cruised down to kiss her nipples through the thin cotton of her nightshirt. Reaching for the hem, he caught it and pulled it over her head, grinning wolfishly as he found her all but naked underneath.

"Maybe I can have a snack first," he whispered, dipping his head to catch one stiff, deep rose nipple in his mouth, drawing the tight flesh inside, and sucking roughly.

Her fingers were busy on his jeans and she giggled, a light, happy sound, as she freed him from his shorts, his cock springing out, hard, thick, a tiny bead of moisture seeping from the tip as she cupped her hand around him.

"You know, we should be tired by now. We should have had enough, after last night," she said, grinning down into his eyes as he dropped to his knees in front of her.

He pulled away, letting her nipple leave his mouth with a wet little *pop* as he sat back on his heels, staring at the pale length of her body, wearing nothing more than a pair of forest green lace panties.

And Tinkerbell slippers.

He grinned at the slippers before he pulled off first one, then the other. Tossing them over his shoulder, he looked at her and smiled. "I won't ever get tired of you, of this . . . I won't ever have enough," he told her, leaning forward and pressing a closed-mouth kiss to her belly. "I could touch you for nineteen hours out of every damned day and still not have enough."

"Nineteen?" she teased. "Why nineteen?"

He grinned wolfishly. "Well, I do have to let you sleep a little."

His hands cupped her ass and he guided her down, staring into her face as she slowly lowered her weight onto him, taking him inside and locking her ankles just above the hard curve of his ass. Eben shifted a little, stretching his legs out in front of him, bracing his shoulders against the wall before cupping his hands around her waist.

He tugged and she slid down, straddling his hips, rising up until only the merest fraction of his length was inside her, and then she pushed down, taking him back inside with one quick, hungry thrust as she covered his mouth with hers.

Eben cupped her ass in his hands and started to pump her up and down, groaning as she wiggled against him, arching her back so that her tight nipples stabbed into his chest. She laughed and grinned at him wickedly just before she started to subtly flex the muscles in her pussy, caressing his cock with slow, maddening contractions. "You're mean," he whispered, dipping his head to catch one rosy pink nipple in his mouth. "Teasing me like that."

She laughed at him, and the look of pure joy in her eyes struck him in the gut like a cannonball. "Think of it as your punishment," she teased, swiveling her hips against his as she continued that internal massage of his dick. Cream flowed from her as she rocked him, and Eben clenched his teeth, swearing as the fiery heat slid down to coat his balls.

"It's hard, but I'll take it like a man," he panted out, lifting her svelte form in his hands, then dragging her back down, shuddering as a spasm tore through her sheath, making her pussy tighten around his cock like a fist.

"Good boy," she teased.

He laughed harshly. "You should have waited before you said that. I'm not going to be good, after all," he told her, just before he rolled, flipping her onto her back and catching her behind the knees, draping her legs over his shoulders. Then he proceeded to fuck her, hard and slow, staring down at her face as her eyes flew wide and her mouth opened in a small O.

He stroked deep inside the tight channel of her pussy, grimacing as she convulsed around him. Her hands fell limply to her sides, her head falling back, lashes closed as her body started to tense and shake under his. "Eben . . . please . . . oh, damn it, please . . . harder, just like that . . . oh, *oh!*" she screamed just before she flew apart underneath him, her pussy gripping his cock like a silken vise, tears sliding out from under her lashes.

Eben growled out her name, slowing his thrusts until he was barely rocking inside her, waiting for her eyes to open again. "I love watching you come," he whispered as she opened her heavy-lidded eyes to stare at him. Then he started to pump inside her, still hard, still aching. "I want to watch it again, and again . . . and again."

Sweat poured from their bodies as they lay on the floor of the small hallway, cold air seeping in from under the door to stroke teasingly along their shifting bodies. Eben arched his back, driving his cock deep and hard inside her, shuddering as she screamed out his name, reaching up and raking her nails across his chest. Hot fiery trails of sensation lingered where she had scratched him, and he burned everywhere they touched, so that his entire body felt like an inferno, just waiting to erupt.

As she once more started to buck and sob under him, his cock buried inside her swollen pussy, the silken, soft tissues convulsing around the steel-hard length of his sex, he came, pumping his come into the fiery depths of her pussy, her name falling from his lips in a hoarse shout.

Later, as she snuggled against him on the floor, he reminded himself they had a dinner to get to. Well, if they were late, it wouldn't matter too much. Joshua would welcome him with open arms, and in time, his wife would hopefully forgive Eben for being a bastard.

But right now, he had all he wanted in the world . . . It was Christmas night, and he had Cara.